**"ARE YOU STILL FRIGHTENED TO LET YOURSELF FEEL, KENDALL? RELAX. I DON'T BITE."**

Drake's voice was a slow, lazy drawl, pitched low to give her a sense of security that she knew was false. Kendall resisted the sweet feel of his fingers on her shoulders and stiffened.

"Oh, Kendall." Her name was a sigh. "I can see you're going to be a challenge, and you know how I feel about challenges."

"Well, then you know I'm a worthy opponent. I believe the score stands at Kendall one, Drake zero."

"But the game isn't over yet." Slowly Drake removed the pins from Kendall's hair until the ebony strands cascaded down her shoulders like a shimmering waterfall. Slowly he combed his fingers through it, absorbing her every feature as his gaze continued its bold inventory for a tension-filled moment. Kendall was rooted to the spot, imprisoned within the cage of his embrace, stunned by her overpowering awareness of his virility, his desire.

*A CANDLELIGHT ECSTASY ROMANCE ®*

162 VIDEO VIXEN, *Elaine Raco Chase*
163 BRIAN'S CAPTIVE, *Alexis Hill Jordan*
164 ILLUSIVE LOVER, *Jo Calloway*
165 A PASSIONATE VENTURE, *Julia Howard*
166 NO PROMISE GIVEN, *Donna Kimel Vitek*
167 BENEATH THE WILLOW TREE, *Emma Bennett*
168 CHAMPAGNE FLIGHT, *Prudence Martin*
169 INTERLUDE OF LOVE, *Beverly Sommers*
170 PROMISES IN THE NIGHT, *Jackie Black*
171 HOLD LOVE TIGHTLY, *Megan Lane*
172 ENDURING LOVE, *Tate McKenna*
173 RESTLESS WIND, *Margaret Dobson*
174 TEMPESTUOUS CHALLENGE, *Eleanor Woods*
175 TENDER TORMENT, *Harper McBride*
176 PASSIONATE DECEIVER, *Barbara Andrews*
177 QUIET WALKS THE TIGER, *Heather Graham*
178 A SUMMER'S EMBRACE, *Cathie Linz*
179 DESERT SPLENDOR, *Samantha Hughes*
180 LOST WITHOUT LOVE, *Elizabeth Raffel*
181 A TEMPTING STRANGER, *Lori Copeland*
182 DELICATE BALANCE, *Emily Elliott*
183 A NIGHT TO REMEMBER, *Shirley Hart*
184 DARK SURRENDER, *Diana Blayne*
185 TURN BACK THE DAWN, *Nell Kincaid*
186 GEMSTONE, *Bonnie Drake*
187 A TIME TO LOVE, *Jackie Black*
188 WINDSONG, *Jo Calloway*
189 LOVE'S MADNESS, *Sheila Paulos*
190 DESTINY'S TOUCH, *Dorothy Ann Bernard*
191 NO OTHER LOVE, *Alyssa Morgan*
192 THE DEDICATED MAN, *Lass Small*
193 MEMORY AND DESIRE, *Eileen Bryan*
194 A LASTING IMAGE, *Julia Howard*
195 RELUCTANT MERGER, *Alexis Hill Jordan*
196 GUARDIAN ANGEL, *Linda Randall Wisdom*
197 DESIGN FOR DESIRE, *Anna Hudson*
198 DOUBLE PLAY, *Natalie Stone*
199 SENSUOUS PERSUASION, *Eleanor Woods*
200 MIDNIGHT MEMORIES, *Emily Elliott*
201 DARING PROPOSAL, *Tate McKenna*

# DANCE FOR TWO

*Kit Daley*

*A CANDLELIGHT ECSTASY ROMANCE ®*

Published by
Dell Publishing Co., Inc.
1 Dag Hammarskjold Plaza
New York, New York 10017



ISBN: 0–440–11662–7

Printed in the United States of America
First printing—January 1984

*To*
*Marcella*

To Our Readers:

We have been delighted with your enthusiastic response to Candlelight Ecstasy Romances®, and we thank you for the interest you have shown in this exciting series.

In the upcoming months we will continue to present the distinctive sensuous love stories you have come to expect only from Ecstasy. We look forward to bringing you many more books from your favorite authors and also the very finest work from new authors of contemporary romantic fiction.

As always, we are striving to present the unique, absorbing love stories that you enjoy most—books that are more than ordinary romance.

Your suggestions and comments are always welcome. Please write to us at the address below.

Sincerely,

The Editors
Candlelight Romances
1 Dag Hammarskjold Plaza
New York, New York 10017

## *CHAPTER ONE*

He intently watched her dancing before him as if she were floating across the stage. She was so graceful that each movement was an illusion of effortlessness. Her beauty was conveyed in every gesture, turn, leap. But he was gripping the arms of his seat to still the rage simmering within him. It had taken a long time to feel ready to confront her again and to demand an explanation. The hurt and anger still surfaced when he thought of the note she had left him. Why had she walked out as if what they had shared meant nothing to her? He had to face her and once and for all sweep her from his mind.

As Albrecht cradled her, she looked one final time into the honey-colored eyes of her beloved. *She had saved him!* She could go to her grave knowing he would live.

As the music swelled to a crescendo and then faded, the curtain fell and the ballet dancers moved quickly into position to take their bows. The curtain rose.

Kendall Lawrence curtsied at the end of her performance of *Giselle* while a tingling awareness ran through her body. As Giselle she had danced beautifully and expertly, as befitted this tragic ballet, but somehow she felt perceptive eyes appraising her and finding something missing. Suddenly her bright smile faltered, and with an effort she fought to restore it.

When an usher handed her a large bouquet of yellow roses, she held it in the crook of her arm and bent gracefully to smell the flowers. Their fragrance wafted into her senses, sparking the ghost of a memory. She loved flowers and her favorite ones had always been yellow roses. Kendall gloried in their sweet fragrance and pushed back the nagging feeling that she had almost allowed to dampen a triumphant moment.

Once again she and her partner, Gregory Spencer, paid homage to the enthusiastic audience, who were offering a standing ovation. As she left the stage, Kendall acknowledged the other dancers' congratulations and made her way toward her dressing room.

Greg placed a hand on her arm as she was about to enter the room. "May I escort you and Cara to Daniel's party?" His hand automatically caressed her arm as his topaz eyes glittered with a suppressed desire for her.

Kendall turned away from the desire in Greg's eyes. She had seen it there too often and she wasn't quite sure how to handle his attention. Greg was a superb dancer and an excellent partner. When they danced a pas de deux, they complemented each other with passion in their steps. But when the ballet was over, the passion fled. Her dancing demanded all of her time and left no room for romance. Suddenly a painful memory flickered in her mind and she frowned.

As she shook the memory from her thoughts, Kendall looked back at Greg, a smile playing across her dark features, her blue eyes gleaming like two sapphires in the morning sun.

"Well, I know my sister is looking forward to this party,

and she certainly deserves to celebrate. Did you see her as Bathilde? I know it was a small role, but one day she'll be a great principal ballerina."

"Like her sister. She has a lot of work ahead of her if she's ever going to be on your level. You were wonderful tonight, but then, you've practiced long enough. When are you going to allow yourself to enjoy the acclaim you richly deserve?"

"Oh, Greg, you of all people know a dancer can never let down her guard. The acclaim would be very short-lived. I'll be ready in thirty minutes." Her smile brightened as she opened the door to her dressing room.

Tonight she had a reason to celebrate. She was at the peak of her form and had never felt better than at this moment. The hard work had all been worth it, she thought, as she looked back over the last eighteen years at the constant rehearsals and classes, the painful muscles, the bleeding toes, and the bitter disappointments when she had lost a coveted role. Kendall had known from the start that the world of a ballet dancer was a world of sacrifices. On stage, though, those sacrifices were forgotten as she became the Firebird, Odile, or Aurora.

As she placed the yellow roses on her dressing table, Kendall noticed for the first time a card stuck in the bouquet. As she slid the card out, one word leaped off the paper, robbing her of breath. The sight of *his* bold, black handwriting made her heart throb with renewed pain.

"Drake!" Her throat closed over the single name.

Momentarily a disturbing and striking vision of him glowed in her mind. After six years he was back in her life. Why? She knew from a weekly news magazine that he had returned two months ago from Europe for his brother's funeral and to take over Taylor Industries. For a fleeting moment she thought of the pain Drake must have felt at the sudden death of his brother. When Drake and she had met six years before, he had often talked of David, his older brother and president of Taylor Industries, headquartered in New York City. Was he now living in New York? Somehow she had never imagined Drake in the city because he had always hated New York, preferring to live in Tulsa.

Why was Drake sending her a bouquet of roses now? She didn't want to see him again. Her feelings for him were dead, she told herself with fierce determination. There were no two people in the world more different than she and Drake. Hadn't she found that out the hard way when they parted?

A knock startled her and she whirled to face the door. "Yes?"

When the door was thrust open, Kendall's breath caught in a gasp and her legs felt like quickly melting wax. She leaned back against the dressing table for support and clenched its wooden top.

"Why are you here?" Kendall strove to keep her voice from quavering, but there was a breathless quality that betrayed her.

"I've heard so many wonderful things about you that I had to come see you dance again." His piercing eyes glinted with a black fire. "I've come to appreciate ballet since the last time I saw you."

He stepped into the room and closed the door. She stood paralyzed, unable to do anything but stare into Drake Taylor's handsome features. They were harder and leaner than they had been when last she had seen him. A lifetime ago, she thought. Cynicism was stamped into those features now, which once had possessed such a bold, reckless smile.

His onyx eyes, which read so much of another's innermost thoughts, held hers captive. With Drake it had always been hard to hide her true emotions, but now she felt it would be almost impossible. With lethal vigor he moved in two long strides across the suddenly very small room to tower over her.

He dominated the room, his muscular build unconcealed by the elegance of his dinner jacket. Suddenly Kendall had an impulse to run her fingers through the unruly thickness of his brown hair with its touches of sunlight. But instead she gripped the dressing table even more tightly and dismissed the foolish impulse.

Moving her gaze from his broad chest to his full, sensual mouth, then finally to his dark eyes drilling into her, she was trapped by his relentless appraisal, caught and bound by the black unfathomable pools that masked his feelings so well. She had once imagined him bluffing his way through a poker game and winning against the odds.

Damn her! She was as beautiful as ever. For six years he had fought her haunting memory, but she had ingrained herself into his life, then had fled, leaving him empty, a part of him dead. Anger sizzled through him. He had always been in control of his life, except for her, and he couldn't forgive her for what she had done to him.

His hard lips curled into an unamused smile as he said, in an infuriatingly placid tone, "It's good to see you again, Kendall. Old friends ought to keep in touch." His casually worded statement was at war with the smoldering fury in his eyes. A muscle twitched in the ruthlessly molded line of his jaw, his features arrogant, savagely noble.

"Never friends, Drake." Kendall controlled her voice to

calmness while the beating of her heart pounded in her ears.

"Ah, yes. I suppose our—relationship was much more intense than mere friendship."

"That was a long time ago. What do you want now, Drake?" An acid ring had crept into her question, for she was stung by the blatant insolence of his survey. "Do I meet with your approval?"

"Very much." The caress in his voice disarmed her. "You've grown much more beautiful, if that's possible, Kendall."

Drake's energy was an almost palpable force as he stepped so close that their breaths tangled. For a moment an enticing smile eased the stark, chiseled lines of his face, and Kendall breathed a little easier—until he slid the straps of her costume off her shoulders and bent to kiss her where the straps had been. Her shock faded, replaced by cold anger at his action. Kendall pulled away only to be hauled against his rock-hard chest. Imprisoning her against him, he kneaded the taut cords of her neck and shoulders.

"Are you still frightened to let yourself feel, Kendall? Relax. I don't bite." His voice was a slow, lazy drawl, pitched low to give her a sense of security that she knew was false.

Kendall resisted the sweet feeling of his fingers and stiffened.

"Oh, Kendall." Her name was a sigh. "I can see you're going to be a challenge and you know how I feel about challenges."

"Well, then, you know I'm a worthy opponent. I believe the score stands at Kendall one, Drake zero."

"But the game isn't over with yet. I only delayed it."

Leisurely Drake removed the pins from Kendall's hair until the ebony strands hung about her shoulders like a shimmering waterfall. He combed his fingers through her hair, absorbing her every feature as his gaze continued the earlier bold inventory of her face for a tension-filled moment.

Kendall was rooted to the floor within the cage of his embrace by her overpowering awareness of his virility. The heat of his gaze stole her breath, and she struggled to drag air into her lungs. She hadn't forgotten Drake's electrifying sensuality; it had always dazed her. In the past she had been confused by the conflict between her intense desire for him and her lifelong goal to be a great ballerina. She couldn't allow that to happen again.

He had wanted to kiss her ever since he had seen her on the stage earlier. Hadn't he dreamed about that enough the past six years? Conflicting emotions warred for supremacy, his overwhelming desire winning for the moment. Surely if he kissed her he would be rid of that dream?

Drake touched the madly leaping pulse at the base of her throat, his thumb making small circles on her flesh. Then his hand traversed her neck with agonizing slowness, slipping beneath the curtain of her hair and tipping her head back. He closed his mouth over hers with a bruising possession that claimed what she had given to no other man. Her lips were parted with a punishing quickness, her mouth probed and explored with a ruthless impatience. Kendall tried to reject his invasion of her mouth, but a wildfire shot through her, banishing any thoughts of resistance. Slowly his onslaught softened, and he seized her lower lip between his teeth and nipped it lovingly. Her senses were spinning as the thrilling seduction of his kiss thawed her and her arms went around him. Buried feelings surfaced to swamp her with a languorous warmth.

Then, without any warning, Drake drew away, placing a few feet between them. The impact of his appearance hit her like a sledgehammer. At the same time his rugged features were twisted into a cynical smile.

"Are you so sure the score is Kendall one, Drake zero?" His eyes danced with satisfaction.

She searched for her own voice, but the combination of desire and anger had stolen it; the words died in her throat. A pallor crept into her cheeks under the disconcerting directness of his look. Aloofness with a touch of predatory ruthlessness was carved into his features. Hostility thickened the air like a heavy fog as their gazes clashed.

"Get out of here before I call the stage manager. Go play your little games somewhere else. *Leave me alone!*" The frosty blue of her eyes hammered into his dark ones. "What we had between us is finished. There is *nothing* now." She arranged her features into an expression of boredom and sent him a patronizing smile.

He laughed, but there was no amusement in the sound. "Is there nothing? You say one thing, but your body says another. Which one is it, Kendall?"

"Nothing has changed. I still have my dancing and that is my number-one priority."

"Did you have a lapse in your priority system a few years ago when you were seriously dating Andre Ruiz? Did you think marrying the principal male dancer of the company would help further your career? What happened to cause you two to break up? Wasn't he able to help you as much as you thought? I seem to remember you became a principal dancer right after you started dating him. Did his usefulness end there? You're at the top now as the best principal ballerina with the best company in the United States." The menacing calm in his voice mocked her.

Fury raced like a searing fire through her. Before she realized it, she had slapped him, her handprint a vivid red on his tanned cheek.

Stepping back from his ferocious look, she said in a low whisper, "Get out now. I don't owe you an explanation. Leave!"

"I'm sorry I bothered you, Miss Lawrence." His cold voice negated his apology.

Kendall watched him leave, the trembling in her hands rapidly spreading through her. *Why had he come back?* He had been the only man to make her want to give up all those years of hard work just to be his wife. For Drake had wanted a wife who would place him first *always.* But at twenty she hadn't been able to give up dancing. She had felt she had her whole future as a ballerina ahead of her.

She closed her eyes, the lids burning with unshed tears. Drawing in a calming breath, she tried to dismiss the sweet memories of those seven blissful months of togetherness. It seemed like another lifetime. So much had happened to them both since their parting. Why hadn't he let the past stay where it belonged?

Kendall came alert at the sound of the door opening.

"I thought you would be ready, Kendall, and you aren't even out of your costume. Greg is waiting for us." Cara walked into the room, shutting the door behind her. "What's wrong?" Worry creased her sister's brow.

Kendall collapsed onto the stool before her makeup mirror, her legs weak, her hands still quivering. "I had a visitor. Someone I hadn't seen in a long time."

"Who?"

"Drake Taylor." His name caught in her throat and Kendall swallowed past the lump.

Cara's blue-green eyes widened. "You haven't seen him in years. Why is he here now?"

"I don't know and I have no intention of finding out." Kendall stood and began to undress. "I'd rather talk about your fine performance as Bathilde tonight. I didn't see one mistake. Don't be surprised if you see your name in the reviews tomorrow, and I know Daniel was pleased. It's a beginning and I'm sure there will be bigger roles soon."

With the subject quickly changed, Kendall forced her thoughts away from Drake, a subject she hoped would not come up again. For her peace of mind she had to keep her distance, but remembering her response to his kiss made her wonder if that was possible if *he* decided otherwise. Could she successfully wipe away all that had been between them—the shared moments, the gentle support? She thought she had, but now she wasn't so sure.

*CHAPTER TWO*

A smile broke across Kendall's face as she sat in the darkness of the taxi. She knew she looked her best in her dress of French blue crêpe with the neckline slanted diagonally across her chest from one shoulder strap, leaving her other shoulder bare. The long, straight skirt was slit daringly up one side, exposing her leg, and around her small waist she wore a silver sequin-studded belt. The dress emphasized her slender neck, slim, graceful body, and dark blue eyes. She wasn't tall, but she appeared to be when dancing en pointe.

When Kendall recalled Drake's visit, her confidence wavered. She thought she had been in control of her life until he walked into her dressing room tonight and stirred up old memories. Her mind raced backward to an autumn day six years ago when a friend had talked her into going to a lake party. It had been one of those rare days when she had allowed herself to rest before rehearsals began for a new ballet for the Tulsa company that she had been dancing with since she was fifteen. The party had been at Drake's family's "cabin" on Grand Lake. That day had marked the beginning of a seven-month courtship in which every spare moment had been spent with Drake.

Anyone else, she supposed, would have been married to

Drake by now, and they probably would have had several children. Kendall couldn't push from her thoughts the memory of Drake's kisses. In his presence she had felt every inch a woman, very desirable and very feminine. Was dancing everything? Should it be her whole life? she wondered rebelliously.

No! She was Kendall Sinclair Lawrence, a principal ballerina with the Manhattan Ballet Company, who, after seeing her first ballet at seven, had decided to become a great ballerina one day and tour the world, dancing with the best.

Soon her dream would be fulfilled and all those years of work would have proved worth it. When she thought about the European tour planned for late summer, she still couldn't believe it was happening to her. Andre had wanted her to be his partner, and they would dance with four world-famous ballet companies in Europe. And this was only the beginning!

"Hey, you two. This is supposed to be a celebration. Where's the lively conversation?" Cara asked.

"That's Greg's department." No more thoughts of Drake, Kendall told herself. He was out of her life *for good*!

"I know one thing," Greg said. "After these last few months of slaving away for ten hours in classes and rehearsals, I'm ready to let loose."

The doorman at Daniel and Margaret's apartment building greeted them with a smile as he opened the door. "Miss Lawrence, I heard you were great tonight. My wife and I are going to see you dance tomorrow night."

"Thank you, John," Kendall replied as she entered the building.

Kendall often visited Daniel Morgan, the company's

artistic director and main choreographer, and his wife Margaret, the company's ballet mistress. She enjoyed the gentle, quiet atmosphere of their home, where a classical composition could always be heard in the background. When she was depressed and wondered if the hard work was worth all she had given up, Daniel was always there to lift her spirits and to help her reconfirm her goal as a dancer. Not only was he a dear friend and excellent teacher, but he also acted as the father she had never known. Daniel kept her straight on the track, firm in his belief that she would be world famous by the age of thirty.

Daniel knew everything about her except for the time she had dated Drake and had been so tempted to forget about her dream. Daniel didn't know that for one month she had been engaged to Drake. At twenty so many things had happened to her. She had become a principal ballerina of the ballet company in her hometown of Tulsa. She had met Drake and fallen in love with a wonderful, kind man who had given her comfort and support when her mother died. Without him by her side during that tragic time, it would have been difficult for her to have continued dancing. But her dream had been her mother's, too, and she had been determined even more to succeed for her mother.

Then the opportunity of a lifetime arose. The Manhattan Ballet Company was holding an audition for a female dancer. Drake hadn't understood her desire and need to try out. He had wanted to get married immediately, before he had to take up his post in Saudi Arabia, but she couldn't have walked away from the opportunity, and end up wondering if she could have succeeded. That would have gnawed at her and slowly come between her and Drake. So she had left for New York.

What would it have been like if she had stayed and

married Drake? Kendall wondered as she handed Daniel her silver-threaded shawl, then kissed his cheek.

"Are you walking on air, Kendall? You should be. Your dancing was passionate. Your lines were clear and pure tonight. I was proud of you."

Kendall smiled brightly. Daniel didn't give a compliment unless the dancer really deserved it. "I always feel on top of the world when I dance. I become a part of the music and the steps flow." Turning to Greg, she took his arm and continued, "But having Greg as a partner makes it easier."

Greg clasped her hand and squeezed it, his honey-colored eyes warm. "You certainly know how to make a guy feel special. But the night was all yours, Kendall. I was only there for support."

Chills flashed up Kendall's spine. She looked across the room and her gaze locked with Drake's. Her heart hammered against her breasts, and it took all her willpower to tear her gaze from his and focus on what Daniel was saying.

"I know I can count on you two," Daniel continued.

"I'm sorry, Daniel. Count on us for what?" Kendall asked, a blush staining her cheeks. She still felt Drake's intense eyes on her, watching her every move.

"I've invited several prospective contributors to the party tonight. Karen thought it was a good idea. She wanted them to meet the company members in a relaxed atmosphere."

Karen Nicholas was the ballet company's financial manager and she was always looking for ways to promote the company. It was expensive to keep the company solvent and Daniel wanted the best. *But this party is anything but relaxing with Drake here,* Kendall thought.

"I want to expand our budget, and of course, to do that I need more money. I want to do more touring in the future as well as another major ballet during the season. We have a damn good ballet company with a great future," Daniel finished with a flourish.

"Is that why Drake Taylor is here?" Kendall had been schooled to appear calm and nonchalant in difficult situations. At this moment, however, she was finding it very hard to appear serene.

"Mr. Taylor has expressed an interest in this company," Daniel answered.

Kendall masked her surprise, but she was stunned. What could be Drake's motive for contributing to the company?

"I bet before the night's through you'll have all the money you want. Perhaps even enough to give Kendall and me a well-deserved raise." Greg's topaz eyes twinkled with mischief.

"The way I feel tonight even that's possible," Daniel said with a robust laugh. "Now, you two go ahead and mingle. Dazzle your fans like you did earlier tonight."

With a glance toward Drake, Kendall inhaled deeply, but her pulse still raced. He was looking at her with an absorbed awareness that she felt could cut through any façade to the truth. She was physically drained after her intense performance and not at all prepared for another confrontation with him. Why had he come to a party he had known she would attend? she wondered. Did he hate her so much that he had to ruin the celebration for her?

Kendall moved across the room from where Drake was standing talking to a tall, beautiful woman. Probably his date, Kendall thought, vividly recalling some of the stories she had heard about Drake since they had parted. When had he ever found time to run the company's overseas operation if he escorted those socialites everywhere the newspapers and magazines had reported?

Greg leaned close to her and slipped his arm about her waist. The gesture was reassuring, as if they were dancing and he was supporting her for a series of pirouettes. Suddenly Kendall felt that before the night was through she would need all the support she could get from her friends.

"What's wrong, Kendall? You're acting strange and withdrawn. That's not like you, especially after a good performance."

"Just tired, Greg."

"Tired? No, that's not it. You've danced *Giselle* many times and never acted this way—not when you danced so well. I know you, Kendall. We've been friends a long time, rehearsing day after day for hours. I saw Drake Taylor leave your dressing room. What did he do to you?" Anger entered Greg's voice as a frown marred his handsome features.

Kendall mustered a smile and answered, "Well, he didn't ravish my body, if that's what you think."

"With his reputation, who knows? He's certainly looks like he hasn't been lonely."

Kendall slanted a glance toward Drake, saying, "Yes, I can see that."

"Was his visit a professional one or personal?"

"Greg, why don't you get me a glass of champagne? As you pointed out, we have a reason to celebrate tonight."

"And mind my own business." Bending even closer, he whispered into her ear, "Kendall, you are my business—that is, if you'd loosen up and let our relationship progress along those lines."

She pulled away. "And ruin a beautiful partnership. No way, Gregory Spencer."

With a sheepish grin Greg stepped back, holding his hands up. "Okay. Okay. You can't blame a guy for trying."

"And trying. And trying!" Laughter trickled through her teasing voice. "No, I don't, but you don't know when to quit."

"That's why I'm such a great dancer. My ambition is bigger than life."

"And your ego. Go get us that champagne."

Greg clicked his heels together and bowed deeply from the waist, sweeping one arm grandly across his body. "I'm forever at your service, madame."

Blushing, she laughed. "Oh, did anyone ever tell you that you're mad?"

"Only my analyst. But then, he's sworn to secrecy. Professional ethics, you know."

With a mock seriousness in her voice Kendall said, "Well, my lips are sealed. I won't breathe a word of this to anyone." Then suddenly a sparkle brightened her cobalt-blue eyes, and a mischievous grin wiped away her serious expression. "I don't think I have to. Your actions speak louder than your words."

"Ah, you wounded me, my sweet." He clasped a hand over his heart, a stricken look spreading across his face.

Kendall darted a quick glance around them. "Shh, Gregory Spencer. These businessmen won't understand your dramatic antics. You'll frighten them away before Daniel has persuaded them to contribute." There was a smile in her voice.

"Maybe if I get you drunk, you'll surrender to my wonderful, dashing male charm."

"It's a waste of your time, but I've heard rumors that a certain dancer with the company keeps eyeing you during class and rehearsals."

"It's that irresistible aura that surrounds me. Which one is it this week?"

Even though there was a light tone in Greg's voice, Kendall heard something else. Was he acting off the stage as well?

"Melinda James."

"Ah, now, she is better than most. I must be losing my touch, though. I hadn't noticed her—interest." Automatically Greg scanned the room and found the principal dancer. "She's certainly pretty." His gaze roamed over her slim body. It had just the right curves in the right places. His eyes rested upon her face with its large, wide-set green eyes, high cheekbones, and straight nose. A mass of blond hair tumbled halfway down her back. Almost to himself he added, "Not bad at all."

"I thought you knew she was definitely interested in you. Be careful, Greg. There's a calculating gleam in that woman's cat eyes."

"Could it be? Are you jealous?"

"No, just concerned that a friend doesn't get hurt."

"Not the company's Romeo!"

Kendall grasped Greg's arm and looked him straight in the eye. "That love story ended tragically. Don't let it happen to you."

"You do care about me!"

"Yes, I do," Kendall said in a low voice, very seriously.

"No frowns, my two stars. Here is some champagne. Drink up *and mingle.*" Daniel handed both of them glasses and moved swiftly away.

Greg lifted his glass in a toast. "Here's to our success.

May we take the country by storm and may your dreams come true, Kendall." In a few gulps Greg had finished his champagne. "I'm going to get another one, then circulate. I wouldn't want to be the one who disobeys an order of Daniel's." Greg walked toward the bar but allowed himself to be sidetracked temporarily by Melinda's delightful charms.

Without Greg demanding her full attention, Kendall felt at a loss. She didn't really want to mingle. She decided to stay only for a while longer, then go home and soak in a hot tub. She walked among the guests, talking and listening but always making sure she wasn't near Drake. She sensed him, however, following her with his intense, probing eyes, and soon the sensation began to weigh heavily. The walls seemed to be closing in on her, and she longed for a breath of fresh air.

Grabbing her shawl, Kendall stepped through the open French doors onto the terrace, the velvet night cloaking her in peace. Faint sounds of the party drifted toward her, and her thoughts wandered aimlessly until suddenly she was remembering the last ballet she had danced in Tulsa. She imagined herself again as the bright, glorious Firebird, half woman, half bird, wearing a brilliant red costume with red feathers in her hair, leaping across the stage as if she were taking flight. Joyously she danced, golden light shimmering around her, the air stirring about her.

Kendall became so immersed in her thoughts that she didn't hear the sound of footsteps. Drake stopped and stared at her as she looked out over the city that was now her home. Suddenly everywhere he turned he saw her, and she drew him to her like a fool toward danger. She was unquestionably very dangerous to him! He had discovered that much this evening in her dressing room. Yet he couldn't walk away. Where she was concerned, it was as if he had no control over his actions, and that disturbed him greatly. He had always prided himself on his cool composure, but perhaps too many things had been left unresolved six years ago. He didn't like loose ends and Kendall Lawrence was definitely a loose end. An inner voice shouted for him to leave. . . .

A hand caressed her arm and, startled, Kendall whirled around, coming face to face with Drake. His musky male scent replaced the scent of a late winter's night. The peaceful moment shattered into a thousand brittle fragments as they stood staring at each other, his features illuminated by the moon, the play of shadows across his face making him seem almost rakish.

Finally he broke the charged silence. "Since the ballet is so important to you, I was sure you would corner me and sell me on the idea of giving the company the money Daniel wants."

The cutting sarcasm in his voice sliced deep into her, the words hurting, his bitterness tangible. "That's not my job," she whispered.

"No. I suppose not. You're a dancer and the idea of helping to raise money might take too much time away from what's so important to you. And nothing must do that."

In a stronger voice she said, "That's right. Even you must realize that in a business each person has his own job to do. Mine is dancing, but you could never accept that, could you?" Her voice held a biting edge that equalled his.

He grasped both her arms and dragged her closer, his mouth inches from hers. "You might like to know that I've told Daniel and Karen that you would be the only one able to convince me to contribute to the company."

Kendall tried to jerk free of his ironclad hold, but his fingers continued to dig into her flesh. "Ballet is my life, but I won't, *I repeat, I won't,* sell myself to you or anyone for it." Fury trembled in her voice; she grew taut and stood perfectly still. "I thought you knew me better than that!"

"I thought I knew you well, too, until you ran off to New York to audition for the company. The worst part of it was that you couldn't even face me and return my ring. You had to leave me a note. Didn't I deserve at least to hear it from your own lips?"

His dark gaze stabbed her, the narrow eyes accusing. She dropped her gaze under his unforgiving stare. She had been wrong six years before in choosing the coward's way out, but she had acknowledged to herself that he held a strange power over her. At the time she had been afraid that he would talk her into giving up her dancing career and going to Saudi Arabia with him. She had felt pulled in opposite directions and confused. So she had run away. It had seemed the perfect solution at the time. But had it been?

Drake framed her face in his large hands and compelled her to look at him. "Answer me! All I did was fall in love with you and what did you do? You threw it back into my face."

Kendall felt the force of his words as if it were a physical blow. His eyes burned into the depth of her being with a relentless wrath. She stared at the lines at the corners of his mouth, lines put there by disappointment and bitterness.

He shook her and whispered his words through gritted teeth. "Answer me, Kendall! Why did you do it to me? I *loved* you. You killed something beautiful and wonderful that day you left me. Why?"

Drake's anger, kept hidden from the world all these years, vibrated through Kendall, stopping the words in her throat.

Drake shoved her away, glaring at her with an unwavering concentration. "Obviously the whole affair was one-sided. You can't even face me now."

Her numbness dissolved as his caustic remarks found their target. "If you had known me as well as you thought you did, you wouldn't have to ask me why. You wanted to take everything away that made me who I was and change or mold me into what you wanted in a wife. I had worked and danced over half my life and suddenly you wanted me to forget about ballet and become your wife and the mother of your children and live in the desert miles from anywhere."

"I would hardly call the capital of Saudi Arabia miles from anywhere. You make it sound like we were going to pitch a tent in the desert alone with no one else around. I was only in Saudi Arabia for two years."

"Two years is a lifetime to a dancer. Most dancers are developing their careers in those two important years. Most dancers don't dance after forty. Their careers are short-lived compared to other professions. That's why I had to audition when the chance came up. You have to work extra hard and take opportunities when they come along because there are so few of them."

"Like Andre Ruiz? Was he one of your opportunities to further that precious career?"

The questions were a slap in the face, and Kendall was so incensed that she couldn't think of a good retort. With one hard yank she freed herself and started toward the

French doors. Drake's hand shot out and spun her around.

"Don't leave when this conversation is becoming so interesting," Drake taunted.

Then with a hard swiftness his mouth swooped down, and his lips ground into hers with a savagery that had a ruinous effect on her equilibrium. His driving possession slowly became a sensuous exploration, a tender search that affected her even more than his punishing kiss. His arms coiled about her, crushing her to him.

He blazed a path of burning kisses to her ear and nibbled, whispering in a husky voice, "Oh, Kendall, why? Why did you leave me? We could have worked things out."

"I know Daniel told us to mingle, but, Kendall, you don't have to carry it that far." Greg stepped away from the doorway, his eyes twinkling. "I'm sorry if I interrupted anything, but Daniel wanted you to meet Drake Taylor. I'll just tell Daniel that you've already been introduced and are getting to know each other—quite well."

As Greg turned to reenter the living room, Kendall slipped from Drake's embrace and walked toward Greg, saying, "Wait up, Greg." She straightened her dress, hoping she didn't look too disheveled. Whether or not she did, Drake certainly had left his mark on her. Her lips felt bruised, her mind a jumble of confused feelings, old ones she had thought had died.

"Not a word of this to Daniel, Greg Spencer. It's my—problem and I'll handle it."

"Sure, Kendall, but if you ever need help, just let me know. I've played plenty of roles where I rescue fair damsels in distress. It could be fun."

Looking around the room, Kendall ignored his offer of help and asked, "Have you seen Cara? I want to let her know I'm going to leave early."

"Want me to take you home?"

"And ruin your chance to score with Melinda! No, I'll take a cab. It's been a long day and I want to be alone."

"Well, I saw Cara around here somewhere with some guy she met tonight. In fact, I think he works for Drake Taylor or something like that. They looked like they hit it off pretty well."

*Works for Drake Taylor!* All of sudden he was back in her life in full force.

"I see her. She's over by the bar." Greg waved his hand toward Cara.

"See you at rehearsal tomorrow. Thanks for bringing me."

As Kendall headed toward her younger sister, she noticed out of the corner of her eye Drake entering the living room through the French doors. He approached his date and whispered something into her ear; then they made their way toward Daniel. When she reached Cara, Kendall was aware that Drake and his date were saying good night to Daniel, and some of the tension that churned within her suddenly left with him.

Sighing, Kendall said, "Cara, I'm grabbing a cab and heading home. You go on and stay. Enjoy the party."

"Fine. Kendall, I'd like you to meet Michael Somers. Michael, this is my famous sister."

Michael extended his hand and Kendall shook it. His warm blue eyes and friendly face made Kendall feel as if she had known him a long time. He had thick, wavy auburn hair and a tall build. He appeared to be in his mid-twenties.

"Nice to meet you, Mr. Somers."

"I'll see that Cara gets home, Miss Lawrence. You don't need to worry." Michael slid an arm about Cara's waist in a very protective gesture that made Kendall like him even more.

"Good. I'll see you two later."

After calling a cab and saying her farewells to Daniel and Margaret, Kendall escaped outside to wait for the taxi. She relished the exceptionally warm winter air and the glimpses of a clear, star-studded sky. Studying the black heavens brought some order to the state of confusion that had possessed her ever since Drake had barged into her dressing room earlier that evening.

Her life hadn't changed. Long ago she had realized that one day she might meet Drake again, since Taylor Industries' main office was in New York. She had thought she'd prepared herself for that meeting, but she hadn't. So she would just have to avoid him. But would she be able to? He obviously felt she had betrayed his love. Did Drake want revenge after all these years?

## *CHAPTER THREE*

"Lift your right leg higher, Kendall. You're too stiff, Greg. You aren't a mannequin. Loosen up, you two. That's it," Margaret shouted above the music to *Summer Breeze,* a new ballet by Daniel.

When Greg and Kendall had finished their pas de deux from Act Two of the ballet, Margaret called out, "You two have earned a short break. Now, let me see Melinda, Jennifer, Mark, and Paul on the floor."

Kendall wiped her brow and neck as she collapsed into a chair by the piano, watching the other dancers rehearse their pas de quatre in *Summer Breeze.*

"She took pleasure in working us extra hard this morning. I think the old dragon didn't like us going to Daniel's party, even if he is her husband."

Kendall heard Greg struggle to catch his breath and laughed. "The old dragon, as you call her, always drives us this hard when we're rehearsing a new ballet. It looks like you had a late night, my friend. Did you finally get together with Melinda?"

"As you've so politely put it in the past, mind your own business. I don't gossip about my love life." The amusement in his eyes took the sting out of his answer.

"You don't need to. Everyone else does it for you." Kendall ran the towel over her face and neck again.

Hearing the door open, they both turned. Even before Drake stepped through the doorway, Kendall sensed his presence and her body tensed.

"Ah, your friend has decided to pay us a visit. Perhaps you were convincing. What I saw last night wasn't a bad start. I noticed that he, too, left the party early," Greg whispered. "Was it because of your wonderful female charm?"

Kendall aimed an angry glance toward her partner. "And you call yourself my friend. I have a good mind to gain ten or fifteen pounds and make it more difficult for you to lift me."

"I'm not so sure all that fine anger is directed at me. Does *the* Drake Taylor ruffle your feathers?"

"I was hoping to catch you all still in a rehearsal," Karen Nicholas said as she and Drake approached them.

Seeing Karen looking so fresh made Kendall even more aware of the sweat that clung to her dance clothes. Karen was so cool-looking in her matching kelly-green sweater and wool skirt—a perfect foil for her dark complexion and black hair. Kendall gripped the seat of the wooden chair, avoiding the gaze Drake was riveting on her.

"I'm showing Drake around and he expressed a desire to watch a rehearsal. I want him to see some of Daniel's new ballet that we're taking on tour." Karen caught Margaret's attention and started toward the older woman, saying, "Drake, I need to have a word with Margaret. I'll only be a minute. Kendall, maybe you could explain the ballet to Drake."

Greg pushed himself away from the piano. "Kendall,

you heard Karen. I think I'll get some water or something like that."

Kendall could have killed Greg gladly at that moment. He thought this was very amusing, but she wasn't laughing.

Anger rose within her and she directed it at Drake. "Quit staring at me. Quit interfering in my life. And quit showing up everywhere I turn around!"

"I thought you were called the ice queen—that is, off the stage. On the stage your fans call you something else entirely, don't they?"

Crimson flooded her face. She knew what was said about her dancing. She had worked long and hard to put passion and vitality into each of the roles she danced. She was anything but an ice queen when she performed.

"Which are you, Kendall? Fire or ice?"

"You'll never find that out."

"Ah, don't be so sure about that. We have some unfinished business, Kendall. And I always complete any task I start."

"I hate to be the one to spoil such a perfect record." Kendall was rising to leave when Karen rejoined them.

"Margaret is ready to go over your pas de deux in the second act again, Kendall. If you want, Drake, we can stay awhile and watch," Karen said.

*But I don't want him to,* Kendall thought angrily.

Greg returned as Drake said, "I would love to, and after this rehearsal I hope Kendall will allow me to take her to a late lunch."

"I'm not hungry."

"Nonsense, Kendall. You should eat something," Greg said, pure devilment sparkling in his topaz eyes.

"You can fill Drake in on the ballet company from a dancer's point of view," Karen added to the argument.

Kendall wondered what Drake had said to Karen earlier. She sensed a conspiracy between them. And Greg, too, had manipulated her into going with Drake. When she got Greg alone, Kendall thought, she would give him a piece of her mind. Surely she wasn't a condition attached to a contribution. Drake wouldn't go that far—or would he? She had been wrong before. She had thought he'd understood about her career from the beginning, but when she'd told him about her chance with the Manhattan Ballet Company, she had found this not to be the case. During their last explosive argument she had made it clear she would continue to dance. And he had made it just as clear that he wanted a full-time wife and a family. Didn't he see that their marriage wouldn't have worked? Or was this merely his male pride talking?

"I don't think—" Kendall began.

"You finish your rehearsal while Karen and I complete a tour of the theater. I'll be back later to pick you up for lunch," Drake interrupted her protest.

If he went now, at least she wouldn't have to endure his watching her learn a new ballet. It was difficult enough without feeling those dark eyes, which could shine with golden lights when aroused, trace her every movement.

As Greg and she went through the steps of their dance for two, she felt like two different people, the dancer and the woman anxiously awaiting a date. She saw herself do a rond de jambe en l'air as if she were a robot programed to perform all the right moves but with no feeling.

"No!" Margaret's cane struck the floor. "No! Do it again. Put some life into your dancing, Kendall," the ballet mistress shouted over and over.

Finally Kendall was able to block the image of Drake from her mind and she concentrated on what Margaret was saying.

"That's it! Lift your head more, Kendall. Jump higher, Greg. Good."

Kendall's movements began to flow—a series of pirouettes, a cabriole, an arabesque—each step melting into the next one. She became emotionally attuned to the music and the choreography and was completely drained when the last note of music sounded in the studio.

"Okay, let's break for lunch," Margaret called out to the group of dancers.

When Kendall stepped into the hallway, she hesitated, looking at Drake standing there with one shoulder leaning against the wall, his arms folded over his chest, his stance calm and relaxed. Somehow she knew he had watched her rehearse from the doorway. She could tell by the smug smile on his face. He was taking immense pleasure in making her feel uncomfortable.

Kendall marched past him and headed for the dressing room, acutely conscious of Drake following her. In her mind she saw his smile widen into a self-satisfied smirk, and her blood was fired.

Whirling around at the door, she snapped, "For the final time, leave me alone! Go to lunch without me!" Her nerves were rubbed raw, and she felt as if her peaceful existence was crumbling.

But he just laughed, saying, "Now, you know I can't leave a beautiful woman alone, Kendall."

"Yes, so I've read." Immediately she regretted that she had read anything having to do with him. A glint sparked his eyes, and she knew he would have a field day with that remark!

"I didn't know you cared so much, Kendall. Well, now I intend even more to take you to lunch."

"I don't have much time. I don't eat much between rehearsals." She was grasping for any excuse, but once Drake set his mind to do something it would take an act of Congress to change his course.

"I know. I remember, but as Greg said, you have to eat something." A teasing gleam sparked his eyes, but under the light tone there was a thread of steel.

Resigned to the inevitable, she sighed, shrugging and saying, "I have to be back in an hour. I'll be ready to go in ten minutes."

Without waiting for a response, she entered the dressing room and quickly showered before she slipped on her jeans and a blouse over a fresh pair of leotards and tights. After toweling her shoulder-length hair semidry, she ran a brush through it, then applied some lipstick. Inhaling a deep breath, she was ready to face him.

Since they didn't have much time, Drake took her to a cafeteria near the theater. After selecting their food, Drake found a table for two in the corner, secluded and separated slightly from the rest of the diners by a partition.

Kendall centered all her attention on eating her salad until, before she knew it, she had finished eating and was obliged to look up at Drake.

"You know, I can afford to buy a date something else besides a salad," he teased.

"I'm not your date. Besides, I told you I wasn't hungry," she retorted, taking a breadstick and eating it.

"Do your actions always contradict what you say?"

She glared at him as she chewed the last of the breadstick and picked up another one. She had to do something to keep herself busy.

"Is that a polite way of saying I lie, Drake? My, you've changed! You used to be so blunt."

"Then, let me put it this way. The way you attacked your salad I thought for a moment you were going to eat the plate, too."

"We came here to have lunch. Nothing more. All I want to do is eat and leave."

After finishing his last bite of lasagne, Drake lounged in his chair. His expression was bland as he removed a cigarette from his pack and lit it. He inhaled deeply; then sent upward a ring of smoke.

Kendall watched the smoke dissipate, then looked sharply at Drake. "When did you start smoking?"

"Six years ago."

"Why?"

"I'm a big boy now, Kendall. What I do with my life is none of your business." Then, as if to emphasize the statement, he drew in again on his cigarette and in a leisurely fashion blew the smoke out.

"You're wrong. I'm breathing the same air you're polluting. If you want to risk cancer, that's *your* business, but smoking around me is *my* business."

Drake roared with laughter. "Please spare me the lectures. Remember, I'm stubborn."

"Oh, you're insufferable, Drake Taylor." She twisted about to watch the people hurrying along the sidewalk. She was willing to do anything not to have to look at him with that roguish smile plastered across his face.

"Kendall, I would like to see you after your performance tonight."

She stared into his dark eyes, which concealed his inner feelings so well. She wanted to say, "No, this is ridiculous," but the words caught in her throat. Something that had flickered for a brief moment in his eyes stopped her refusal. It was starting all over again. She could feel him slowly casting his spell over her and she felt helpless to stop him. Why did he hold such power over her? Was it because she knew of the great tenderness he could express? His gentleness after her mother's death had been the balm she had needed so much then.

Suddenly it was as if those years had never occurred, and she was frightened. Yet, at the same time, she was intrigued by the memory of the intense feelings of the time so long ago when she had been in his embrace, his mouth softly caressing her neck. He had heightened her awareness of everything around her and had added a depth and passion to her dancing.

"Why?" she finally whispered.

"Because I want to see you, Kendall. As I told you before, things aren't over between us—not by a long shot, babe."

Her heartbeat accelerated at the use of the word *babe.* He had said it many times during the months they had dated. He said it still in the same gentle tone, as if he were caressing the word. *Oh, my God! I'm losing!*

"No!" she said in a harsher voice than intended.

But he merely smiled, a smile that was dangerous to her emotional state. He took her hand in his, and his thumb made slow circular patterns on her palm.

"Why not?" Drake asked in a very enticing voice.

"Because—I don't think I need to answer that. You know, Drake." A shiver streaked up her arm and moved through her.

"All I want to do is take you to dinner. Where's the harm in a dinner date?"

The sensuous look in his eyes was her undoing. She

could remember that same look entering his eyes and the way it would make her feel—very womanly and very desirable—and found herself saying, "Okay, Drake. I'll go, but just this one time."

He stopped the torturous movement of his thumb, but her hand stayed within his. "Good. I'm interested in what's been happening to you—since we last met. Obviously you've done quite well as a dancer, but then you always had the drive and ambition to get what you wanted."

He didn't have to add, "So much drive and ambition that you gave up marriage and a life with me." But she knew that he had thought it. It showed in the hardening of his eyes, the slight clenching of his jaw.

Drake relinquished his hold and stood. "I'd better get you back." His tone was suddenly very businesslike.

At the theater he leaned across the taxi and opened the door, saying, "I'll pick you up at your dressing room after the performance."

As Kendall watched the taxi pull away from the curb, she could feel again the caressing movement of his thumb on her palm. His mere touch made her heart pound, made her legs feel like ice on a hot summer's day. This time she wouldn't run away from her feelings or from him. She would face them head on and conquer them. Running away hadn't solved the conflict, only delayed it. Before it was over, he would understand she was above all a dancer.

Kendall made her way toward her dressing room with another bouquet of yellow roses cradled in her arms, its sweet fragrance tantalizing her.

"Kendall."

Kendall stopped and faced her sister. She was glad she

wasn't Cara's age of twenty again. She could still remember being in the corps de ballet and the long, strenuous battle of becoming first a soloist, then a principal dancer, and finally arriving at the top, with Daniel creating ballets especially for her.

"I won't be coming home right away tonight," her sister said, her blue-green eyes shining with anticipation.

"Oh? A date?"

"Yes. You remember Michael Somers? Well, I'm going to a late supper with him."

"Don't forget we have an early class tomorrow morning."

"Yes, mother dear," Cara said with a laugh, then hurried toward the corps de ballet's dressing room.

Kendall quickly removed her heavy stage makeup and undressed. It would be just like Drake to appear immediately after the performance. She heard a knock at the door not a minute after she had dressed in red satin pants and was slipping the long-sleeved, red satin tunic over her head. She fumbled with the zipper in the back, and in her haste it became stuck. Cursing, she thrust the door open, hoping it was anyone but Drake.

Drake grinned down at her. "Having trouble?"

"Can't you give a person a chance to get dressed?" she snapped, exasperated at the expression of pure joy on his face.

"Maybe I can be of some help. In my vast experience I've rescued a few ladies when their zippers became unreasonable and refused to budge."

"I'm sure you have," Kendall muttered as she turned her back to him and allowed him to work the zipper free.

But after freeing the zipper, instead of easing it up, he brushed her bare neck with feathery kisses, then pushed the tunic off her shoulder and trailed kisses as soft as a gentle breeze across her back to her neck.

For a shattering moment Kendall was frozen, unable to do anything but thrill at the provocative feel of his warm lips on her skin. Then, as if someone had counted to three and snapped his fingers to bring her out of her hypnotic trance, she yanked the tunic back up and put the distance of the dressing room between them. She shakily slid the zipper up and smoothed the satin material in place, avoiding Drake's smoldering gaze.

"Where are we going to eat?" Kendall finally asked, in control now, as she brushed her hair, letting it hang loose.

"It's a surprise. A new place that just opened," he answered.

When she had finished dressing, she turned toward Drake and asked, "I'm not too dressed up, am I?"

"No, you're just fine, babe." His low, throaty voice tilted her balance, its rich tone meant to seduce her.

"Drake, before we go tonight, let's get one thing straight right at the beginning. It's been a long day and as usual during the ballet season, I'm tired. This will have to be a short evening."

"When do you find time to relax and enjoy life, Kendall?"

The question caught her off guard, and she couldn't think of an answer for a long moment as Drake's eyes bored into her.

"I don't think you need to answer, Kendall. You have a very expressive face that no doubt is a great asset to your dancing." Drake reached out hesitantly and ran his hand lightly down her jawline.

Her heartbeat quickened as she looked deeply into the

blazing depths of his eyes and felt lost, burning in the swirling inferno.

"Life is more than having a career. Even with my busy schedule I always find time to play and enjoy life."

"That's great for you to say. Your career will last way into your sixties while mine will probably end in ten or fifteen years. Remember, a dancer's performing career usually is short." She dragged her gaze from his and bent to pick up her purse. "You grab what you can when you can. Besides, Drake, I *enjoy* dancing. And I do take time out to relax. Now, I'm hungry. I think I could put two dinners away."

Later, as Drake drove toward Central Park, Kendall asked, "When did this restaurant open?"

"Tonight."

"Oh, then you don't know much about the place."

"I know the chef is excellent and I can guarantee the service is great."

Kendall laughed. "How? Do you own the restaurant?"

Instead of answering her, Drake pulled his car into an underground parking lot to an apartment building.

"Is this where the restaurant is located?" Suspicion sounded heavy in her voice.

"Well, actually, it's where I live."

"Drake Taylor, take me home immediately!"

He turned the engine off, then twisted around to look at her. "Are you afraid, Kendall? You shouldn't be. Nothing will happen tonight, I promise—unless you want it to. My chef is excellent and Alfred is a good butler. You'll hardly know he's around when he's serving."

"Okay, I'll sample your chef's food, but *that is all.*"

"Of course, that's all I expected." But the mocking tone in his voice refuted his statement.

What did he want from her? Kendall wondered. Revenge? To make her fall in love with him all over again, then leave her as she had him? Had she ever fallen out of love with Drake? Had she really loved him as a twenty-year-old with a lifelong dream within her reach? Didn't love conquer all?

Confused thoughts rolled through her mind. Kendall didn't know the answers to those questions, but she felt she would find out in time. One thing was certain. Drake was back in her life for better or worse, no matter what his reason was.

When Kendall stepped into the spacious foyer, the beauty of Drake's penthouse greeted her. To the right was a winding staircase that led to the bedrooms on the second floor and to the left was the large formal living room and dining room.

Alfred appeared from the back of the penthouse and asked, "Would you like dinner served now, sir?"

"Yes. Tell Marianne we're ready to eat, Alfred."

"Marianne?" Kendall's brow furrowed.

"My chef. Would you like to meet her?"

"Leave it to you to have a female chef. Did you bring her back with you from Europe?" Flashes of magazine articles about Drake and his lady friends filled her mind.

"Actually Marianne was David's chef for two years before he died."

Suddenly Kendall felt an inch tall and instantly regretted her question. She placed a hand on Drake's arm and said, "I'm sorry about David's death. He was too young to die from a heart attack."

"He *enjoyed* his work so much that the stress and strain finally got to him. He didn't know how to relax, either. He ate, slept, and talked Taylor Industries. He never even found time to get married and have a family. I won't let that happen to me." His voice was hard, his bitterness evident. "I'm the last of the Taylors and it's up to me to keep the family going."

Drake had moved away from the touch of her hand and turned his back on her. But she didn't need to see his face to know of the pain in his dark eyes. David and Drake had been five years apart in age but had been more than brothers. Drake had worshiped his older brother. The shock of his sudden untimely death must have been a crushing blow. She now wished she had been with him to help ease the hurt, but she had been away on tour at the time. When at last she had found out about the death from a weekly news magazine, a week had passed since the funeral. She had sent flowers immediately but hadn't received a reply or heard from Drake until the other night.

When Alfred reappeared to announce dinner, Drake's features were neutral, and all the pain in his voice was gone. Again Kendall marveled at the way he could hide his true feelings. To be a successful businessman she guessed it was necessary. But his withdrawal left her not knowing where she really stood with him, Kendall thought as Drake escorted her into the dining room.

The room, with an antique oak table that seated fourteen and a glittering massive chandelier that hung over the middle of the table, was impressive. The table, polished to a high sheen, was cozily set for two at one end. Drake pulled out a high-backed chair, and Kendall sat on the rich gold brocade seat. Memories of other nights spent eating an intimate dinner with Drake moved through her thoughts, and she felt as if she were going back in time.

After Alfred poured the white wine, Drake lifted his glass in a salute and said, "Here's to your success, Kendall. I, of all people, know what it means to you." There was a sharp edge to his voice.

"I'm not so sure you do, Drake. I believe that was part of our problem in the past. You wanted me to give ninety percent to the relationship and settle for your ten percent."

For an endless moment Drake leveled a hard look at her, his hand clenching his wineglass, his eyes like black flint. "When do you go on tour?" His face was void of any expression now as he sought to change the subject.

"In a few weeks."

"Where will it take you?"

"To Boston, Philadelphia, and Washington."

Drake finished his wine in several gulps, then refilled his glass. "Will you be gone long?"

"Three weeks. Why the sudden interest?"

"I'm interested in everything you do, Kendall. *Everything.* Why should I donate money to the ballet company? What do I get out of it? Can you convince me it's worth it?"

Kendall rose and stared down at him. "If you have to ask, then my answer won't satisfy you. The arts obviously don't mean much to you. It's hard to put a price on culture."

His mouth twisted into a sardonic smile. "Oh, I don't know about that. I just bought an expensive Monet."

"Take me home, Drake." She hated the desperate ring that crept into her voice. "It's been a long day, and I don't care to spend the evening fencing with you."

"I have no intention of taking you home until you sit down and at least sample Marianne's wonderful culinary creations. Now, there's an art." Drake stood, towering over her, the blackness of his eyes challenging her.

Too tired to argue anymore, she sat down. When he began to speak again, she tensed, expecting a further discussion of her dancing. But Drake surprised her by talking about his company's move into the energy field and their research into alternate sources of energy. The energy division of Taylor Industries was expanding rapidly, becoming the company's greatest asset.

Then he directed the conversation toward some of his experiences at the Saudi Arabian court and later to some of his escapades in Europe. By the time dinner was over, Kendall was relaxed and was enjoying their light conversation, which had placed no strain between them.

After eating her chocolate soufflé, Kendall leaned back. "I'm stuffed. I don't think Greg will be able to lift me tomorrow at rehearsal. My compliments to the chef."

"Why don't you tell her yourself?" Drake asked, rising and pulling Kendall to a standing position. "Come on. You can at least move, can't you?"

Laughing, she replied, "I'm not so sure. I haven't eaten this much in ages."

"Well, then, there is only one course of action left for me."

Before Kendall realized his intention, Drake had swung her up into his arms and was carrying her toward the kitchen.

"Put me down, Drake Taylor. What will Marianne think?" she asked, still laughing. A memory of the first time he had carried her in his arms played in her mind. They had been swimming at Grand Lake and, exhausted, she had declared she couldn't make it up the slope to his house. He had carried her all the way up the hill as if she weighed no more than a feather, then had proceeded toward the bedroom. . . .

"Probably that I've wised up. She will be overjoyed that I'm finally dragging my woman off to . . ." His voice faded into the silence as their gazes touched.

Kendall's arms coiled around him, the memory of that first time engraved vividly in her thoughts. Pausing, Drake brought his mouth down on hers in a gentle mating that ignited a deep response in her.

When he drew away and trailed kisses to the sensitive cord of her neck, she moaned, "Oh, Drake," delicious sensations pushing all thoughts of resistance from her mind.

Instead of entering the kitchen, Drake headed for the winding staircase. Kendall laid her head on his shoulder, breathing deeply of the pine-scented aftershave lotion that mingled with his distinctly pleasant male odor. She belonged in his arms. The feel of them about her was so natural, so right. It was impossible for her to forget those times they had shared, the closeness that had bonded them together.

When he had shouldered the door to his bedroom closed, she lifted her head and surveyed the masculinely decorated room with Drake's personal touches evident in the Monet, the oil derrick done in bronze on his dresser, and *a picture of her by his bed*!

But before she could ask about the photograph, he had laid her on his king-size brass bed and was staring down at her. The smoldering passion that blazed in his eyes trapped her, making her devastatingly conscious only of him. Easing down next to her, Drake smoothed her hair away from her face. He looked reverently and deeply into her eyes, silently asking her if she were sure. She answered him by winding her arms around him and pulling him even closer to her. There was an emptiness inside her that only Drake could fill. All of a sudden she realized that not even her dancing could give her complete contentment. Dancing couldn't touch that one small part of her that was shouting its need. But Drake could.

He brushed his lips across hers; then his mouth traversed her neck to the hollow at the base of her throat, lightly kissing her. His hand meanwhile moved under her tunic, then up to cup her breast. He lifted his head, a look in his eyes that promised completely delightful satisfaction.

He cradled her face within his powerful hands, his rapt expression extolling her loveliness. "I've dreamed of this moment for years, babe." His voice had a deep mesmerizing tone that seduced her even as his eyes magnetically held her.

When he opened his mouth over hers again, she felt as if his potent power had entered her bloodstream, sending an electrical current through her. She could only cling to him and revel in the closeness of the moment, something she had hungered for but denied herself for so long.

Drake rose to undress, breathing in quick, shallow gasps. A smile broke across Kendall's face at the sight of him standing over her in proud nakedness, a warmth encircling her throat as she took in his tall, beautifully proportioned frame. She inhaled deeply to calm the galloping of her heart, but an intoxicating breathlessness attacked her lungs, making each breath labored.

Drake leaned down and pulled her tunic up and over her head, then unfastened her satin pants and slid them down her body, her underwear quickly following her clothes to the floor. Straightening, he ran his hand over her breasts, and her senses danced at the light touches of his fingers. His raking gaze missed nothing as it traveled over her, leisurely, maddeningly, delighting in the provocative curves of her body. His searching fingers adored her while his eyes worshiped her, arousing her beyond the limits of time and space and transporting her into another realm.

Kendall opened her arms wide and welcomed him into her embrace, quivering as her body came into contact with the hard expanse of his. He feathered kisses to her earlobe and nibbled before his mouth descended on hers in a hungry, demanding union.

She felt his carefully controlled passion in the way he built slowly but steadily upon each mind-shattering sensation he created until her nerves screamed with yearning.

"Drake, don't torment me so," she whispered, her voice husky with desire.

But he ignored her plea and continued his exquisite torture, his mouth returning to coax her even further toward a rapturous experience, toward a world where her senses dominated, where rational thoughts were impossible.

He moved to her breasts, rolling a nipple between his lips, his tongue flicking it into a hard point. Then he repeated the teasing action with the other nipple while shudder after shudder rippled through her.

Kendall gloried in the feel of his muscular back and in his overwhelming sexuality. Small whimpers of pleasure escaped her. She pressed him more intimately to her soft contours, returning his kisses with her own fierce claim.

"I can't leave you alone as I did six years ago, Kendall. Not now."

"I don't want you to. Please don't."

Drake's hand went lower, brushing across her flat stomach, then slipping between her legs to tantalize them open.

A burning awareness of his every move sent heat spreading to all her nerve endings as if it were the sun rising and its rays were fingering out in all directions.

Drake eased down on top of her and filled the aching void within, moving in an agonizing slow pace, finally increasing his tempo as the storm he had carefully and painstakingly built burst and raged through her. They came together in a mutually overpowering climax that left them joyously exhausted, each savoring the moment of total fusion with the other.

Drake collapsed upon her, pleasurably heavy, his ragged breathing sounding in her ear. Minutes passed as they gathered themselves together, marveling in their complete surrender.

Then Drake rolled off Kendall and pulled her to him, burying his face in the silky strands of her hair, his breathing still uneven. When she turned to look at him, Drake touched her mouth with his, fleetingly at first, then with such intensity that air wouldn't penetrate her lungs.

"You're mine, Kendall. I won't let you go this time. No man can make you feel the way I do. You aren't free of me, babe."

She stiffened and tried to pull away, but he wouldn't release his masterful hold, which suddenly was like a prison.

"Are you so sure?" There was a taunt in her voice, for she hated that possessive satisfaction in his.

"Yes. You may lie, but your body doesn't."

Finally she managed to free herself and she sat up. "You forget a good ballerina must be an accomplished actress."

Hurt burrowed deep into her. He was turning this beautiful experience into a contest of who would dominate whom. She sought for a way to strike back, to hurt as he had.

Catching sight of the picture of her dressed in the Firebird costume on the bedside table, she asked, "Are you so sure I'm the prisoner? Why do you keep a photograph of me by your bed? Is it the last thing you see before you go to sleep at night and the first thing you look at in the morning?"

He bolted up in bed and forced her head around to look him straight in the eye, his fingers digging into her jaw. "Actually I keep the picture of you there as a reminder never to love a woman so completely that when she walks out of your life, you feel so empty inside that no one can fill the void. If you had stayed long enough, Kendall, I'm sure we could have talked things through." Releasing his hold, he rose to dress. "Frankly, I don't give a damn now. It took a long time, but I've finally exorcised you from my system. You no longer have the ability to hurt me. You're beautiful to look at, but that's all!"

With all her strength Kendall fought back the tears. He acted as if she had walked away from him unscathed when in reality she had been in a hundred different pieces. The slow rebuilding of her life hadn't occurred overnight, and now she realized it wasn't complete even today. But listening to him, there was no doubt about the contempt he felt for her.

Had she been so young and inexperienced when she first met him that she hadn't given him a real chance? Hadn't Margaret told her many times to experience life in the fullest and not to make dancing her whole existence? She and Drake had argued about her ballet career before she had left for the Manhattan Ballet Company's audition, but perhaps she had given up too soon.

Her mind throbbed with those unanswered questions. If she had made a mistake about Drake all those years before, she couldn't change it now. She had to live her life today, making the best of what she had. She couldn't allow Drake to see that he had gotten his sweet revenge. Pride wouldn't let her.

Sliding from the bed, she gathered up her clothes and headed for his bathroom. At the door she turned back toward him and asked in a cool, calm voice, "Have I convinced you to contribute to the company?"

Then, without waiting for an answer, she entered the bathroom and closed the door. Trembling, she leaned into the vanity for support. Never before had she seen such a murderous look on his face. His gaze had impaled her with his scorn.

## *CHAPTER FOUR*

Drake and Kendall rode to her apartment in complete silence. As soon as Drake pulled up in front of her apartment building, she hurriedly threw open the car door and climbed out without a backward glance at him.

Kendall was relieved that Cara wasn't up when she returned to their apartment. She felt dead inside and couldn't face talking with her younger sister. All Kendall wanted to do was crawl into bed and sleep—for days.

After undressing and getting into bed, though, she just stared at the ceiling, watching the shadows, imagining them to be Drake laughing at her, glaring at her with a look that could kill. Even when she squeezed her eyes shut, he haunted the darkness. She couldn't rid herself of him!

Kendall rolled over and pounded the pillow. Damn him! Determinedly she shoved him from her thoughts and ran through the new ballet of Daniel's that she was learning. She was the wind, dancing light and airy steps. Then she became a tornado, wreaking havoc as she whirled across the stage. Slowly as she danced the ballet in her mind, she drifted toward sleep and completed the pas de deux—with Drake. . . .

"Kendall. Kendall! Wake up!"

Her name filtered through the haze of sleep clouding her mind, beckoning her toward wakefulness. Opening her eyes halfway, she moaned, "Go away, Cara."

"Kendall, I can't believe *you've* forgotten about our class today. It's earlier than usual."

Kendall struggled to sit, propping herself up on her elbows. "What time is it?"

"Eight. You have forty-five minutes to get ready. I'll fix us something to eat."

As Cara left her bedroom, Kendall swung her legs to the floor. This morning her body refused to cooperate. She moved as if she hadn't danced in a month as she went into the bathroom to shower. When she came back into the bedroom, she dressed slowly in faded jeans and a red pullover sweater. After placing her tights, toe shoes, and leotards into her nylon dance bag, she sat at her vanity table, where she tried to make herself look presentable. After carefully masking the circles under her eyes, she walked into the kitchen.

The smell of coffee and toast turned her stomach. She always ate a light breakfast, but today she didn't even want to eat a piece of toast or a boiled egg. She knew she should, since she rarely ate much during the day with her busy schedule. Drake had certainly turned her world upside down!

"Have a seat. I have everything under control," Cara said as she stood at the stove.

"I think I'll just have some orange juice."

Cara paused at taking the boiled eggs from the stove and faced Kendall. "Are you sick? You've been acting very strange lately. Maybe you'd better stay home today. Remember, you have a performance tonight."

"I don't have to be reminded I have a performance," Kendall snapped, then immediately regretted her curt tone. "I'm sorry, Cara. No, the last thing I need to do is stay home alone with my thoughts."

"You went out with Drake last night. I was back here at one, and you still weren't home. During the season you never stay out late, especially when you've danced that night. Do you need someone to talk to?"

"There isn't anything to talk about. What Drake and I had once is over—*definitely over.* Instead of talking about me, I want to hear about your date. Do you like this Michael Somers?"

Cara's blue-green eyes lit up, and a smile brightened her features. "Oh, he's wonderful, Kendall. So kind and considerate. I've never met anyone like him."

"Cara, you haven't dated many men. Be careful."

"Kendall, quit trying to be my mother. At twenty I've dated more men than you had by that age. We're going out again tonight."

"Don't—" Kendall caught the sharp look that entered Cara's eyes and swallowed her advice. She had to let Cara live her own life, but it was hard to let go, especially when she saw her sister making some of the same mistakes she had.

"Cara! The toast is burning!"

Cara whirled around and removed the two burnt pieces, laughter bubbling from her throat. "Well, thank goodness you aren't very hungry."

For the remainder of the breakfast Kendall steered clear of the subjects of Drake and Michael. Instead they discussed Daniel's *Summer Breeze,* in which Cara had a soloist part.

"It won't be long before your roles will be bigger. I think Daniel and Margaret have a lot of faith in you. I know I'm proud when I see you dancing with all eyes trained on you," Kendall said as she rinsed the dishes and handed them to Cara to dry.

"I suppose a lot of people don't have ways to express themselves creatively."

"We're lucky we have our dancing. When I'm on the stage dancing, I put my whole self into my role. It's an exhilarating feeling that's hard to explain to someone who hasn't danced." Immediately Kendall thought of Drake and the times she had tried to tell him of her need to dance. *She had to stop thinking about him!*

"Are you looking forward to Andre's returning soon? Have you heard from him since he started filming the movie?" Cara asked.

"Yes to both questions. But what I'm really looking forward to is the European tour this summer."

Cara picked up her bag and headed for the front door. "He's such a dynamic, exciting dancer. I can't wait to see him in that movie." Pausing at the door, she faced Kendall. "What I don't understand, though, is why you two have never become serious. Even when you dated a few years ago, neither of you was serious."

"He's too much of a friend. Besides, I could never see myself romantically involved with my teacher, and between Andre and Daniel I've learned so much in the last six years."

"They saw your gift and helped you develop it. I wonder, Kendall, if things are over between you and Drake." Cara's brow creased in a thoughtful expression. "Could you become romantically involved with Drake again? I know things didn't work out before, but . . ."

"No. Drake will not become a part of my life again," Kendall answered forcefully.

But later, halfway through her morning class, thoughts of Drake still plagued Kendall. She was doing everything wrong. Her turnouts weren't good. Her jumps were sloppy. She couldn't seem to muster the concentration she needed to perform the movement phrases. It was hard to shake the depression that was settling in. A dancer should give all, but there just wasn't all of her there to give. Part of her was still with Drake. Maybe it had always been like that, and she had been kidding herself when she thought she had gotten over him. Was that why she hadn't encouraged Andre? Drake accused her of using Andre to get ahead, but she hadn't. Very quickly she had realized that no one would take Drake's place in her heart—not even someone as talented as Andre. He was one of the top male dancers in the world, and she admired him a lot. But she couldn't bring herself to be anything but a friend and partner to him.

"Kendall! Obviously your mind isn't here today. You're wasting our time," Margaret said in a very quiet voice.

"Sorry, madame. I'll do it over." Kendall danced the steps again, but lost her balance on a turn.

"Again," Margaret said patiently.

Focusing all her attention on her body, Kendall finally performed the dance steps perfectly.

"That's better. Work on it some more," Margaret commented, then turned to watch Melinda.

When Melinda had finished, she paused next to Kendall and, with a smug smile on her face, whispered, "Are you losing your touch? Perhaps you shouldn't dance tonight.

I could always play Giselle."

"The part of the cold, wicked Queen of the Wilis is more befitting to you, Melinda," Kendall said before walking away, anger in her strides.

That woman wanted her place in the company and would stop at nothing to get it, Kendall fumed silently. She was going to have to try harder to erase Drake from her mind, or she was going to find herself no longer a principal ballerina with all the roles she wanted to dance. There were always a lot of dancers waiting for her to fail so that they might take her place. She always had to stay in excellent condition and strive to do even better than she had in the previous night's performance. And Melinda was very good.

Kendall's temples throbbed and her neck and back were sore. The last several nights she had forgotten to stretch her muscles before going to bed, and she felt tight as a bowstring.

After the morning class Cara asked, "Come to lunch with Michael and me, Kendall? I want you to get to know him. You don't have a rehearsal till much later."

She didn't feel like eating, but her sister rarely asked her to do anything, so Kendall agreed. After changing into their street clothes, Kendall and Cara met Michael outside the theater at Lincoln Center. Cara greeted Michael with a kiss; then he circled his arm around her waist, drawing her to his side.

Flashes of the past ran through Kendall's mind. She could remember Drake waiting for her after a class, then putting his arm about her shoulder as if he were declaring to the world that she was his. The heaviness in her chest made each breath difficult. It was hard to look at Cara and

Michael and not see herself and Drake as they had been. Would it end the same way for Cara? Kendall prayed it wouldn't.

Kendall managed a smile and forced a cheerfulness into her voice as she asked, "Where are we going?"

"To Michael's apartment. He loves to cook and has promised us a great lunch."

"Are you sure you want your old sister to tag along?"

Michael grinned. "Yes, this was my idea. I thought I should get to know Cara's sister and vice versa."

Gazing at the looks exchanged between Cara and Michael, Kendall's fears were confirmed. This was no casual affair. They were very serious—and after knowing each other only a few days!

"Well, I'm glad you like to cook, Michael. After the burnt breakfast Cara fixed me, I could use some nourishment."

Kendall liked Michael's apartment. Decorated with simple, modern furniture, the living room was done in different shades of brown with navy-blue accents. From his picture window Kendall had a glimpse of the Hudson River.

"Have a seat, ladies. I'll check on lunch, then be right back."

When Michael had left, Cara turned to Kendall and asked, "Isn't he terrific? He's forever doing wonderful little things for me, making me feel very special and very much a woman. I've never felt this way before."

Cara didn't have to say the words "I love him," but they were there in her voice. How would Michael feel about Cara's dancing career? Kendall wondered. A lot of men couldn't or wouldn't compete with a woman's career. Then came the nagging doubt that maybe she had decided for Drake and hadn't given him a chance to make up his own mind. Could she have persuaded him about the audition and dancing with the Manhattan Ballet Company?

"Go slowly, Cara. It's a wonderful feeling being swept off your feet, but you'll come down to earth one day. I wouldn't want it to be a crash landing."

"You're just full of motherly advice today. Well, for once I'm going to give you some, Kendall. Melinda is after your job, and after your performance in class today, she's one step closer."

"A person is entitled to a bad day every once in a while. Do you think I would allow someone like Melinda to take my roles away?"

"You may not have a choice in the matter if *you* aren't careful. You drive yourself too hard. Take some time off for yourself. In the long run it will help your dancing."

A frown wrinkled Kendall's brow. "You sound like Drake."

"Then, he has a point. Whatever is bothering you isn't going to go away overnight. This isn't just one day that you've been out of sorts."

Kendall breathed a sigh of relief when Michael picked that moment to reenter the living room. "Lunch is on the table, ladies. I prepared a Mexican chicken dish especially for you, Cara. I know how you love Mexican food, and this is one of my favorites."

Michael seated first Cara and then Kendall before serving the main dish. When Kendall sampled the chicken dish, she commented on its delicious flavor, then fell silent for the rest of the meal while she ate a small portion. She would be dancing in a few hours and didn't want to eat too much.

She felt out of place and self-conscious as she tried to

ignore the hand-holding and the "eyes only for you" look that Cara and Michael shot each other. Kendall wished she hadn't come. Seeing them only made her ache for Drake and what could have been if she had been someone else.

At least Kendall found out that she liked Michael and was glad that Cara was dating someone who treated her so well. Special. Womanly. That was what Cara had said. A lot like the way Drake had treated her when they had been dating. Was it possible that underneath that hard shell Drake still had feelings for her? Would it be possible to break through that armor of steel he wore? Did she even want to?

She was so preoccupied with her own thoughts that Kendall almost missed what Michael was telling Cara on the ride back to the theater.

"I won't be able to see you tonight after all. I was lucky to get this lunch break. Drake's leaving late this evening for two weeks to visit the overseas office, then take a vacation." Michael smiled, an impish look appearing in his eyes. "I think he's meeting a certain lady friend for a cruise of the Greek islands. He never said anything, but the office gossip . . ."

Meeting a lady friend! Well, that ought to be her answer, Kendall told herself. But wouldn't it be wonderful to take a few weeks off and cruise the Greek islands with Drake? What difference did it make to dream about a trip like that? First of all, he hadn't asked her, but some other woman. And second, she couldn't have gone even if he had asked. The company was leaving on tour in less than four weeks and she had a new ballet to learn for its première in Boston and the other cities on the tour.

* * *

Daniel sat on a stool in the dance studio and observed Kendall and Greg rehearsing his new ballet. Kendall was too tight. She was depressed and anxious over something. He could hear it in her voice and see it in her face. If she didn't watch out, she would injure herself. He had postponed having a talk with her, hoping whatever had been bothering her this last month would take care of itself, but the company was going on tour in two days, having finished their New York winter season three weeks before, and he wanted Kendall ready with his *Summer Breeze.*

A frown cut the age lines deeper in Daniel's face. He sensed that Melinda's presence was upsetting Kendall, but she was a pro and had been a principal ballerina with his company for over three years. She had what it took to make it to the very top, and competition from other dancers in the past had never bothered her.

Daniel got to his feet and walked toward Margaret. "I think we should take a break."

Collapsing on the floor and leaning against the wall, Kendall took her towel from the barre and mopped the sweat from her face and neck. She had felt today as if she were coercing her body into each dance step instead of flowing from one to the next. And worse yet, her turns weren't right. She was coming off point.

"Kendall, I would like a word with you before you leave," Daniel said in a businesslike voice.

She stiffened, her muscles tightening. A shot of pain tore into the calf of her leg, and she nearly cried out. She massaged the soreness and slowly worked the knot of muscle loose.

"You aren't relaxing properly. This just proves what I was going to talk with you about." Daniel offered to help her stand. "Now, young lady, what has been bugging you that you can't leave it at home?"

"My performances have been fine."

"Yes, I can't complain. I've seen better, but I've also seen worse. What concerns me is the way you're pushing yourself with learning this new ballet. I choreographed this one with your assets in mind. The female lead is perfect for your abilities. You aren't using all your senses to learn it properly. Feel the music and the steps, then just do it. Quit thinking so hard about it. That's not how you learn a new role."

"I know. I can't clear my mind. I'll work on it. I'll be ready by the time we go on tour. I haven't failed you yet. I won't this time, Daniel."

"Kendall, you're keeping something from me. You never used to do that. Does it bother you that you won't be partnered with Andre in *Summer Breeze*? You and Greg look good together. In the future Andre's career will take him more and more away from the company."

Kendall slung the towel around her neck and began walking toward the door. "No. Greg is a good partner. I appreciate your concern, Daniel. If it weren't for you and Andre, I wouldn't be where I am today, but there are some things a person has to work out for herself."

He stopped her with a hand on her arm and she faced him. "Are you having doubts about your commitment to ballet? Many dedicated dancers do when they reach your level and age. It's natural, Kendall. You have great potential and I want you to achieve the very top."

Tears misted her eyes. Daniel had always been there for her as a supportive friend and she was shutting him out. But how could she voice all the doubts she'd been having since Drake had reentered her life? She couldn't to Daniel, the one motivating drive behind her career. She hadn't seen Drake or heard from him, but he was constantly in her thoughts as she moved through the day. She felt like a puppet being manipulated by him, and she resented Drake's intrusion into every facet of her life, especially her dancing, until she couldn't even perform to her potential. Since that night at his house she was even more determined to erase him from her mind. *Then, why was it taking so long?*

"Thanks, Daniel. Don't worry about me. I'm tough. Dancing is my world." She forced conviction into her voice.

"Good." Daniel glanced at his watch. "Oh, my Lord, I'm late. I've got an important business meeting. If this goes well, we'll have all the extra financing we need for my plans."

A shiver tingled along her spine. She had to ask, "Who are you meeting with?"

"Drake Taylor and Karen Nicholas. If Mr. Taylor contributes, I owe all the thanks to Karen. I think she's been the reason behind his sudden interest. As our financial manager, she can be quite persuasive, not to mention the fact that she's single, beautiful, and charming."

Kendall's mouth was stretched into a tight smile that threatened to falter. And Karen was also a rich socialite who didn't need to work and would make a perfect wife for Drake, Kendall thought. Karen would be an ideal hostess who would always devote the right amount of time to her charities but have plenty of time left over for Drake.

Jealousy made Kendall rigid with inner tension, and her voice didn't sound as sincere as she had wanted when she replied, "I hope she was able to convince Mr. Taylor. I've heard he's a hard businessman and not very interested in the arts."

"When I talked with him last week, I didn't get that impression. I hope your information is wrong. Got to run. See you after the rehearsal this afternoon."

Kendall watched Daniel hurry down the hall, a frown marring her beautiful features. It had been three weeks since he had left for Europe, so Drake had been back at least a week from the cruise and hadn't called her. But then, what had she expected after their last confrontation?

"If it's the last thing I do, I *will* forget him," she muttered as she headed for the dressing room.

As she was taking a container of yogurt from the refrigerator there, Cara burst into the room, her face aglow. Kendall glanced over her shoulder as she finished pouring a glass of milk and said, "I could use a ray of sunshine today."

Cara thrust her left hand toward Kendall. "Michael just proposed to me! What do you think? Isn't it gorgeous?"

"Beautiful, Cara, but isn't this a little sudden? You two have only known each other for a month."

"What's time got to do with it when you know you love a man and he loves you? That's all that matters."

"Is it?" Kendall sat on a bench and kneaded the calves of her legs. A slight soreness remained in the calf that had cramped.

"What's that supposed to mean?" Cara's voice had sharpened. "I should have known you wouldn't be happy about this. You expect me to be just like you. You expect me to give up all else, so I'm left free to dance, to become a principal ballerina. That's old-fashioned, Kendall. A lot of ballerinas, good ones, marry, and some are even having children now."

Kendall stopped massaging her leg and stared up at Cara. Her sister's eyes narrowed and her hands were on her hips as if she were ready to fight the world. "I know marriage is fine—for some, but not for all. And of course, it all depends on the man a dancer plans on marrying. He has to be able to share her with the world, with her *very demanding* career. Their life wouldn't be normal. A ballerina goes on tour and is gone a lot. Is Michael ready to accept that? Does he really understand what your life is like?"

Cara lifted her chin in a defiant gesture. "Yes, he does! He loves the ballet and wants, in fact, encourages me to continue my training and my career if I want to."

"Then he is a rare man, and I have nothing else to say except I wish you all the luck in the world."

Cara sat next to her on the bench. "Oh, Kendall, do you? That means a lot to me. You're the only family I have."

"When do you two plan to get married?"

"Sometime soon. Maybe after the company returns from our tour."

"Why the rush?" As soon as Kendall asked the question, she wished she hadn't. Cara was certainly old enough to make her own decisions—and mistakes. She couldn't help the love she felt for her younger sister. She didn't want her to get hurt, and hurrying into something as serious as marriage might lead to some grave problems later.

"You're never going to change, are you, Kendall?" Cara blew out an exasperated breath of air. "Why wait? We know what we want to do and postponing it a few months won't make any difference."

Kendall bit her lower lip to keep from making a reply.

"I'd better eat this lunch, then get back into the studio. These muscles need an extra-long warm-up today. How's the corps doing? Any problems?"

"Not big ones. Of course, Melinda is working very hard on her variation, as you well know. She gloats over the fact that she was recently made a principal dancer. Never lets the corps forget."

"Nor me," Kendall said, then began to eat her plain yogurt.

"There's something else, Kendall."

The wary tone in Cara's voice made Kendall look sharply at her sister. "From the sound of your voice I'm afraid to ask."

"Michael asked Drake this morning to be his best man and he accepted. They've worked together and been friends since Saudi Arabia. In fact, Drake insisted on giving us an engagement party when we return from our tour."

Kendall gritted her teeth and nearly crushed the plastic yogurt container. *Get out of my life, Drake Taylor,* she shouted silently.

"Kendall, I know there are some hard feelings between you two, but Michael really wanted to ask him. I thought at least for our wedding you two could call a truce."

"Don't you worry about Drake and me. There is no way I would spoil your wedding. Now, if I'm going to be prepared for this new ballet, I'd better get moving."

Later, as Kendall walked toward the studio, she saw Daniel, Drake, and Karen coming toward her. A smile froze on Drake's face as his eyes glinted. They passed her in the hallway, heading toward Daniel's office, Daniel and Karen greeting her while Drake remained stonily quiet.

From the look on Drake's face, nothing had changed

from their last meeting. Watching them enter Daniel's office, Drake casually guiding Karen, Kendall felt sick and tired. The strenuous workouts and the emotional strain of Drake's reappearance into her life were having their effect. Something would give soon if she couldn't unravel the emotional tangle she found herself trapped in. Everywhere she turned, Drake was there, almost as if he had planned his revenge step by step and now was carrying it out with great pleasure. If he ever knew she still had deep feelings for him, she would be lost. If nothing else this last month, Kendall realized she still loved Drake, that her feelings for him had never died. But even if Drake still loved her, a marriage between them would be impossible. They were too different, their lives were going in opposite directions. Six years hadn't changed that.

## *CHAPTER FIVE*

Taking her bows with Greg at the Kennedy Center, Kendall noticed a man approaching from the wings with a bouquet of yellow roses. Her smile vanished for an instant as she took the roses; then, hearing the thundering applause, she smiled again at the audience, but her eyes no longer sparkled.

As she and Greg left the stage, he whispered, "From that secret admirer again. Yellow must be in this season."

"Since you seem to like them so much, you can have them. I've had my fill of yellow roses." This bouquet was the third one she had received on the tour—all from Drake, one in each city. What was he trying to do to her?

Greg bellowed with laughter. "Don't get mad at me. I didn't send them. I think I'd better take my exit before you want to give me more than those yellow roses. I've felt the sharp edge of your tongue before. I can forego that experience." Greg bowed deeply from the waist and began to back gallantly away.

"Hold it, you two," Daniel called out as he neared them. "After you get dressed, there's a buffet for the whole company at Drake Taylor's hotel suite."

A boyish grin spread across Greg's mouth and he

looked sideways at Kendall. "Is it a command performance?"

"No, but a free meal is being offered afterward," Daniel answered.

"And on a dancer's salary, you'd be crazy to pass up such a fine offer," Greg said, his gaze again directed toward Kendall, an impish gleam in his eyes.

Her mouth formed a tight-lipped smile. She wouldn't allow Drake to play his little games any longer. The best way to put an end to them was to go to the buffet and act as if he meant nothing to her, that his presence didn't send her heart slamming against her breasts. Ignoring him and getting on with her life would be the best thing to do. But the only thing wrong with that was that Drake was impossible to ignore. He had a physical magnetism that kept her looking at him even against her will.

"I'll be ready in a few minutes," Kendall said. "Who can decline Drake Taylor's *kind* invitation? I'm sure he has only the best."

"I'm sure he does, too," Greg teased, making it clear he didn't mean food.

Sending Greg an annoyed look, she said, "If you two gentlemen will excuse me, I wouldn't want to keep Mr. Taylor waiting."

Inside her dressing room, Kendall proceeded to remove her heavy stage makeup and her costume, soft and flowing like the wind she had played. She had little to choose from, since she hadn't brought much with her on the tour. At least she had worn a nice dress to the center tonight thanks to that reporter who had wanted to interview her.

After showering and blow-drying her hair, Kendall slipped on the beige batiste dress with a full skirt and scooped neckline. She inspected herself in the mirror as she tied a sash around her slender waist. After carefully applying brown eye-shadow, an apricot-colored lipstick, and light powder, she arranged her hair by sweeping it back on one side and placing a tortoise-shell comb in her hair to hold it. She would make sure she looked her best. Drake wouldn't have the last word in this matter!

Kendall accompanied Daniel and Greg to the party at a plush Washington hotel. Drake greeted them at the door to his suite with Karen at his side. Kendall's heart skipped a beat at the sight of Drake dressed in a dark suit that made his eyes seem even blacker, more menacing, as he turned and insolently looked her over. His gaze told her that he meant to exact further payment tonight for what she had done all those years before.

Lifting her head higher, she returned his look boldly, silently daring him to try. Outwardly she was calm and cool as she shook hands with him, saying, "It's kind of you to invite the company tonight." The polite words were spoken with a hard edge to them.

"Will you be glad to return to New York tomorrow?"

"Yes. We have a new ballet to learn and that's always exciting." They were talking as if they were two strangers who had just met.

"I'd hoped I could persuade you to fly back with me on my plane. We have so much to catch up on." Suddenly an intimacy had entered his voice, and this time he silently dared her to accept the invitation.

"Why, thank you, Mr. Taylor. I think I will."

The surprised look that flashed in his dark eyes told her that he hadn't thought she would accept. She smiled inwardly. She had said yes on an impulse and now she was glad she had. She rarely threw Drake off guard and it felt wonderful.

"We will leave at nine tomorrow morning."

"That's perfect. I can be back in time to take an afternoon class at the studio," Kendall said, then sauntered away, very aware that Drake's penetrating eyes were following her.

Minutes crawled into an hour, and Kendall sought for a way to escape the party. She had been through the buffet line but had eaten very little. Everywhere she looked she saw Drake, with Karen often next to him. Playing the unconcerned role was making her weary. A tour was always exhausting and demanding with strange theaters to dance in, cold hotel rooms to return to each night, and the local press who wanted to interview her between the rehearsal and the performance when she should be resting. It would be nice to be back home tomorrow, but now she regretted having accepted Drake's offer. He had a way of disarming her defenses, then going in for the striking blow when she was most helpless.

"I'm sorry I've neglected you, Kendall," Drake said mockingly, "but as the star of the company you're used to everyone's attention, so I didn't think you needed mine, too." As he sat down next to her on the couch, his thigh touched hers, sending a stunning bolt through her.

She moved to place several inches between them. "I wouldn't want to take you away from your other guests. Please don't worry. You haven't neglected me. In fact, the party has been rather pleasant—until now."

"Is that any way to talk to your host? I spent a lot of my valuable time arranging this little party."

Kendall leveled an angry look at Drake. He had a way of getting under her skin with one sentence. "Why are you in Washington?"

"To see Daniel's new ballet. Ballet is becoming more

interesting every day. In fact, I've decided to make a sizable contribution to the company."

"Oh, how nice," she replied harshly.

"That doesn't sound grateful."

Kendall stood and stared down at Drake. "Who convinced you? Karen or me?" Then she pivoted and walked away from him. That infuriating, pigheaded . . .

Steel fingers clasped her elbow and halted her escape. Drake's grip tightened painfully on her arm as he swung her around to face him. "Jealous, babe?"

"I'm not your babe," she answered in a whisper, the words almost a hiss.

"Aren't you?" His gaze traveled over her, devouring her, telling her he knew the secret places to touch her and ignite the flame of her desire. "Do you want me to give you the credit for my decision to invest in the company? Will that make you feel better? I hear dancers sacrifice a lot for their careers, but until I met you, I hadn't realized how much."

Kendall dug her fingernails into the palms of her hands. She was itching to slap that smirk from his face, but that was what he wanted her to try so he could further humiliate her in front of the company. She wouldn't play by his rules.

She smiled sweetly at him and curled her body into his. "We all must do our part for the good of the company. I try to do my best to help out where I can."

His mouth was pulled into a tight smile. "I'll have to remember that when Karen wants more money." Then he extracted himself from her and strode away.

Relax, Kendall told herself. But each muscle was pulled taut, and she felt that if Drake said one cross word to her,

her muscles would snap. Glancing across the cabin in Drake's Learjet, Kendall watched him busily working on some reports, not having spared her a second's notice since he had told her to have a seat by the window. He had dismissed her with those curt words—or rather that order—as if she were his employee.

In a way Kendall guessed she was, now that Drake was a major contributor to the ballet company and Daniel was placing him on the company's board.

"A political move," Daniel had told her this morning.

Bored and restless, Kendall flipped through a current magazine, but the words blurred before her eyes. Couldn't he at least acknowledge her existence on the plane? Couldn't he say something? Anything! Irritated at herself and Drake, she practically threw the magazine back on the table.

"My, my, are we in a temper this morning," Drake mocked. "Is the service on this plane lacking?"

"What service?"

Grinding out his cigarette, Drake closed the folder in front of him and stood, stretching, and then coming around from behind the desk. "As your host, I've neglected you again. I'll try to make up for that oversight." He sat down in the chair next to hers and took one of her hands within his, his thumb stroking the palm of her hand. The gesture was meant to unnerve her and succeeded. "A definite oversight. I must have been mad to work with you sitting across from me."

A thrill rocketed through her at the tantalizing huskiness in his voice. Now that he was here talking to her, she wished he would go back to his reports. He could devastate her with a simple smile and make her senses scream for more than his touch. And worse yet, he knew it! She could read it in his eyes. She could hear it in his voice.

"Now, babe, how should I make it up to you?"

She felt as if she were a mouse and Drake were a cat, playing with her, teasing her right before he went in for the kill.

"I don't need you to entertain me. I've done quite well without you." Her voice sounded so breathless, and she felt so warm with Drake only inches from her.

"I shall let those remarks pass, Kendall."

His raven-dark eyes with golden glimmer bored into her. Amusement no longer lit them, but desire did. Kendall tried to pull her hand away, but he just tightened his hold until it was painful.

Drake cursed himself for having invited her to travel back with him. He had tried to ignore her on the plane and had succeeded until she threw down that magazine. He had looked over at her and had become lost in the midnight blue of her stormy eyes. The dull ache inside him had intensified, and he knew it would be useless to work. He doubted he had accomplished much anyway. Blast her! Why couldn't he get her out of his system? Why was he constantly comparing every woman he met with her? He knew he would always come second in her life and that hurt his male pride but, worse, his heart. Why had he come to New York? After his brother's death he could have moved his main office to Tulsa, where he preferred to live. No, he'd had to see her again to prove she meant nothing to him. And look at him now sitting next to her like some lovesick schoolboy. Damn the woman! Damn her dancing!

"Drake, you're hurting me! Let go of my hand!"

Drake looked at their clasped hands and saw the death

grip he had on hers. He pushed her hand away as if it had burned him. Hadn't that been what she had done to him six years before? She had left him scarred, unable to find total happiness with any other woman—but most of all with her—and that was unforgivable.

Drake managed a relaxed pose as he stretched his long legs out in front of him. "Would you like me to drop you off at your apartment or the dance studio?"

"Neither."

He cast a questioning glance at her. "Oh? I thought you would be eager to go straight to the studio."

"And are you going home or to the office? No doubt to the office. So why should my job be any different?" A fire illuminated her blue eyes as angry sparks flew at him. "But what I meant was I would get my own ride home. I don't want to be in your debt anymore."

"Then why did you agree to come?"

"I'm beginning to wonder that myself. Maybe I thought we could talk about Tulsa and what happened to us—calmly and rationally. But I can see it would serve no purpose."

As quick as a jungle cat springs at its unsuspecting victim, Drake pulled her to her feet and imprisoned her against his whipcord strength, one hand tangled in her hair as he forced her head back. Her eyes were fastened on his ruthlessly molded features.

"You don't think I could let that challenge pass. Oh, no. I must see that this trip is worth it to you. Perhaps I should offer to increase my contribution. Would that make you happy?"

Anger surged through Kendall. She tried to struggle free of his embrace, but she only managed to pull her blouse from her pants and to work the top two buttons loose. Drake's gaze moved lower until it rested upon the firm roundness of her breasts. The amusement in his eyes was quickly replaced by desire as his look consumed her inch by scorching inch.

Drake stared deeply into her eyes, communicating his desire for a long moment before he crushed his lips into hers, prying hers open with his tongue and plundering her mouth to taste the sweetness within. His hand traveled slowly down her blouse, unfastening each button until the blouse fell open. When he cupped her breast, she found herself lost in the blissful sensations he could always create. Kendall arched her body toward him, all thoughts of their past or future swept from her mind by the tidal wave of primitive longing that swelled within her. She wrapped her arms around him and clung to him as his kiss deepened.

"Oh, Drake, love me now," she murmured as she nipped at his ear, tunneling her fingers through the brown richness of his hair.

He swept her up into his arms as if she weighed nothing and headed for the rear cabin. "I'll have to have the captain go on to Boston. I wouldn't want you to miss out on a membership in the mile-high club."

His words pierced the velvet mist that was shrouding her. Underneath the teasing, light tone there was a hard thread in his voice.

"Mile-high club?"

"You're entitled to membership if you make love a mile up in the air."

"I see. Are you a charter member?"

Her passion turned into rage as his mouth lifted in a sardonic smile. This was just another one of his games—just another way to pay her back! Her rage began to boil rapidly as she remembered how she had practically begged him to make love to her.

"Put me down, Drake. I don't have time to belong to a club." Each word was snapped out between clamped teeth. "Remember my dancing?"

Without any warning he released her, and she nearly fell to the floor. She caught herself on a chair while he just stood and watched her. Steadying herself, she faced him with defiance in her narrowed eyes.

"Don't you ever come near me again, Drake Taylor. I won't be used by you or anyone." She advanced on him, her body strained with anger, her arms rigid at her sides. "Do you understand?" Her voice rose as she spat out each word. Raising her arms, she hammered his chest with her balled hands. "I won't have it!" She punctuated each word with a blow that he seemed to take with amusement.

Finally deciding he had had enough, Drake seized her wrists and held her arms still, his fingers bruising her flesh. "Are you through with your—assault?"

Kendall wrenched herself from his hands and backed away, fighting the tears that had lodged in her throat. He had the power to hurt her deeply and her heart already ached with painfully increased beats.

"No! I will admit I did some wrong things in the past, but leaving you wasn't one of them!" Her breasts heaved as she drew in deep breaths. "I *will not* spend the rest of my life paying for something you think I did to you. Can't you be man enough to walk away and leave me alone to live my own life? Haven't you done enough these past few weeks?" She swallowed away the tightness in her throat and boldly matched his steadfast gaze.

An icy hardness crept over his features, and Kendall

was immobilized by the cold savagery of his stare. His fury pulsated through him and transported itself to her.

"I was thirty when I met you and had done my share of hell-raising, Kendall. But you made me want to give all that up. I had loved my life-style until you came along and showed me how empty it really was. But that was all you did. You gave me a glimpse of how my life should really be, then you moved on. How do you think I should feel when you took part of me and stomped all over it? I vowed that that would never happen again."

His attention deliberately wandered to her breasts, still exposed to his mahogany dark eyes that were shimmering with his mixed emotions. Contempt won and he dragged his gaze away, turning from her.

"Get dressed, Kendall. We'll be landing soon and I wouldn't want anyone to get the wrong idea."

The caustic bite of his words knifed through her. She fumbled with the buttons, but her hands were trembling so much that she couldn't manage them. With a curse Drake crossed the cabin and shoved her hands away, fastening the buttons himself, quickly, as if her nearness was offensive. Then he pivoted and walked to his desk, where he buried himself in paperwork.

Somehow her quivering legs supported her long enough to allow her to sit and buckle herself in. She stared unseeing out the window, her thoughts in a riot. Until now she hadn't realized all the hate that Drake felt toward her. It trembled through her like a living force. For the first time in her life she wished she had never seen the *Nutcracker Suite* as a child of seven. That was when her dream of becoming a world-reknowned ballerina had begun. What would she have been like if she had never put on toe shoes? Would she have married Drake and been happily content with him and a family? She couldn't answer those questions. She couldn't turn back the clock. *She wouldn't!*

Finishing her series of grand battements, Kendall placed her right leg on the barre and stretched toward the raised leg. After the stretching exercise, she moved into the center of the studio with the other class members.

When she had arrived in New York the day before, she had come to the dance studio to try to work off some of her frustrations. Falling into bed last night, she had been exhausted but wide awake. She had tossed and turned most of the night with images of Drake dancing before her eyes. Her frustrations had only mounted and nothing she did made them vanish.

While Kendall berated herself for letting Drake get to her, the class was doing a series of steps with a turn and a grand jeté. Kendall leaped into the air for the grand jeté and came down wrong, landing on her right foot at an angle that sent her toppling over. Pain shot from her ankle up her leg, and she instantly knew she had injured herself—and all because of Drake Taylor!

Margaret knelt over her and examined her ankle. It was sore to the touch. Kendall gritted her teeth and tried to block from her mind the stabbing pain.

"It looks like a sprain, Kendall. We'd better get you to Dr. Olsen," Margaret announced.

Greg and Paul helped Kendall to stand, then supported most of her weight between them as they escorted her to the dressing room.

"Your mind was a thousand miles away, Kendall," Greg said in the hallway. "You can't let him interfere with your dancing. If this ankle is only mildly sprained, you'll be lucky, my dear. A dancer's body is her livelihood. Think of him when you're in bed at night, not in class."

"I don't need your lectures, Romeo."

Greg was nearly as angry at her as she was herself. It wasn't Drake's fault. It was hers. She should have been able to bar him from her mind while she was working. But how do you block anyone as utterly male and dynamic as Drake from your thoughts? Kendall asked herself.

An hour later she listened to the news that she had dreaded to hear. "Kendall, it's sprained and you'll have to stay off it for about two weeks, then slowly begin to work again. If it hurts at all, stop until it's completely healed or you'll do worse damage than a mild sprain. Do I make myself clear?"

"Yes, Dr. Olsen."

"Good. You dancers sometimes try to start working too soon after the injury and only end up seeing me again. Now, go home and apply a cold compress while elevating that leg. Keep the ankle wrapped and avoid doing too much, especially walking, for the next day or so. Tomorrow you can begin applying heat to your ankle twice daily."

When Kendall reached her apartment, she thanked Greg for his help, then sent him back to the studio. She followed Dr. Olsen's orders to the letter. She had been foolish to injure herself in the first place. She wouldn't make two mistakes and not care properly for the aching ankle.

But the hours moved slowly for Kendall as she sat with her leg propped up, staring at the television. Even though the season's funniest television show was on, she couldn't find anything to laugh about. This afternoon the company had begun to learn a new ballet, and she would miss at least two weeks of rehearsals. The company was to perform *La Valse* at their April performances. Would she have time to learn her role?

The front door opening brought Kendall's head around. Cara and Michael walked into the apartment, sadness etched into their features.

"My injury isn't that bad," Kendall tried to joke.

Not even a faint smile flickered across their faces. Cara sat while Michael paced back and forth.

"We have something to tell you, Kendall, and I'm not sure how to break the news," Cara said.

Kendall sat up straight, the sudden movement causing her ankle to throb even more. "What's wrong? Has something happened to Drake?" Now, why had she asked that?

"Michael is being transferred to Alaska for two years."

"Alaska! Two years!"

Michael halted his pacing. "The company is having some problems with its oil fields in Alaska, and I'm the one elected to straighten them out."

"Who elected you?" Kendall asked, her heart pounding. She knew who had. Drake.

"Drake," Michael calmly answered.

"I'm sorry, you two. I wish you didn't have to postpone your wedding, but maybe it won't be for two years."

"It doesn't make any difference, Kendall, because I'm going with Michael. He leaves at the end of next week, and I'm getting married to him in three days."

"No! You can't. Your dancing career!" Kendall turned her beseeching gaze on Michael. "You can't let her give up her career. It's only for two years."

Cara stood. "Michael, I'll see you tomorrow. I want to talk with my sister alone."

After Michael had left, Cara said, "Kendall, I know it

will be hard for you to understand, but Michael is my life. Without him my dancing wouldn't mean anything. I love to dance but not as much as you. I think part of the reason I started in the first place was to be just like my big sister. Besides, I'm not giving it up completely. I'll teach, then, when we return, I might dance professionally again."

"Cara, I can't believe I'm hearing this. Would you stop if Drake wasn't sending Michael to Alaska?"

"No, not for now at least. But the fact still remains that Drake is sending Michael to Alaska."

Kendall struggled to her feet, putting most of the pressure on her left leg. "We'll just see about that." She hobbled toward the phone and called Drake's penthouse.

"I thought you had said all you wanted to say yesterday, Kendall. I'm busy. What do you want?" Drake asked testily.

"To see you." Somehow she managed to keep the anger out of her voice, but her hand clamped the receiver so tightly that her knuckles were white.

"Me! A summons from the snow queen herself!"

"Perhaps the fire has thawed her."

"I have—an engagement—in an hour. I'll stop by before it."

Kendall refrained from slamming the receiver down. She had to remain calm.

"Cara, I'd rather you not be here when Drake arrives."

"Fine. I'd just as soon not witness World War III. But I must warn you, Kendall, that Drake, according to Michael, isn't a man to reverse a decision easily once made. He doesn't take any of his commitments lightly and Taylor Industries is a big commitment."

Her sister's words echoed through Kendall's mind the whole time she impatiently waited for Drake. By the time she made it to the door, he had rung the bell three times. Obviously he was impatient, too. With whom was he going to spend the evening?

"Come in." Trying to avoid any physical contact with him, Kendall opened the door wide, leaning on it for support.

"What happened to you?"

"A mild sprain. You'll be relieved to know I'll be back dancing in two weeks."

"Oh, I'm glad to hear it was nothing permanent. What would you do without your dancing?" Sarcasm was heavy in his voice.

"Then, why are you taking my sister's career away from her? Did you decide to send Michael to Alaska to get back at me?"

"Don't flatter yourself. I made a purely business decision that had nothing to do with you or Cara. I had been considering Michael before they announced their engagement. Believe it or not, this is a good promotion for him. We worked together in Saudi Arabia and I know he can handle the problems." Why, he asked himself, was he standing here explaining everything to her? He didn't owe her anything!

All of Kendall's calmness slipped away as she faced Drake, her eyes shining with her wrath. "Cara and Michael are getting married in three days, and she's going with him. Where you're sending him there isn't much but snow and ice. My sister has a great talent that you're denying her."

Drake exploded. "*I'm* denying her! It looks like she's made her own decision. I'm glad for Michael that she's going with him. He's lucky. He'll come first in her life. Let your sister make her decisions without you adding your two cents' worth."

He advanced until his hot breath mingled with hers. She could see every angry line in his features. She could see his jet-black eyes flame with his fury.

"Have you ever stopped and thought, Kendall, that maybe Cara isn't as obsessed with her dancing as you? That maybe she wants more out of life than just her career?"

"And you think by sending Michael to the ends of the earth that you're giving my sister her chance?"

With a look of disgust he turned away. "You're impossible. You won't understand it isn't good to be so single-minded. What will happen when you can't dance anymore? What if that injury had been permanent?"

"That won't be your problem. I know better than anyone my years are limited. That's why I'm asking you not to take away two of Cara's best years from her—please." She almost choked on the last word.

"It seems I've heard that plea before—six years ago, to be exact. But my decision stands. Michael goes. For your information I've already talked to *both of them.*" Drake walked to the door and placed his hand on the knob. Throwing a glance over his shoulder, he continued, "The wedding will be at my penthouse Thursday afternoon with a dinner afterward for the bride and groom before they leave on their honeymoon to Mexico. You're welcome to come, of course." Then he opened the door and left; the sound of its closing was very final.

Kendall stared at the door for a long moment until her eyes stung with her unshed tears. When she blinked, a lone tear slid down her cheek, and she wiped it away furiously.

She allowed him to keep coming back and hurting her. Would she ever be rid of him? She should hate him, but she couldn't. He was doing enough hating for the both of them. The hurt twisted deeper into her heart.

## *CHAPTER SIX*

Kendall paid the taxi driver, then limped toward the double doors that led into the building where the dance studio was located. This was the first time she had visited the studio since her injury a few days before and she was now questioning the wisdom of her decision. She couldn't dance, so why torture herself with watching others? Because her apartment was so lonely and she found herself very bored an hour after she got up in the morning.

Turning at the door, she looked up and glimpsed patches of clear, bright sky between the towering buildings. At least the day promised to be a beautiful one for Cara's wedding, even though in Kendall's heart she felt her sister was making a mistake and rushing into marriage with Michael. But no matter what she had said to Cara over the past few days she knew her younger sister would be standing before the minister this evening in Drake's apartment and exchanging vows with Michael.

As if it were the day before, Kendall could remember the mind-stunning sensations that encased her when Drake held her close, caressing her with a gentleness that she hadn't thought possible from him. It was hard for her to reconcile the image of the man she had known six years before with the man now. The aura of command that surrounded him had always been there, but now there was an added dimension, a wiry toughness that gave the impression of lethal force.

With a deeply felt sigh Kendall moved to enter the building, making her way to the elevator. The company dance studio was on the third and fourth floors of the building.

When the doors swished open, Kendall inhaled another soothing breath, then started down the long hall toward Studio One, where Greg and some of the dancers would be rehearsing *La Valse.* Rehearsals would be early today so the dancers going to Cara's wedding would be able to attend later in the afternoon.

As Kendall entered the studio she was conscious of her aching ankle, again emphasizing in her mind her inability to dance for another week. She still wasn't able to walk very well and when she did it was with a slight limp. If only Drake hadn't come back into her life, she wouldn't be slowly going stir-crazy with nothing to do for two whole weeks.

Kendall eased into a folding chair along the wall, propping up her injured leg with an elastic bandage around the ankle in another chair in front of her. And what am I going to do when Cara leaves? she wondered. If she thought the days were crawling by now, she realized she would be in for a worse time tomorrow and the next day and the days following that.

Damn you, Drake Taylor! Why couldn't you have left me alone?

Kendall tensed, but her expression registered no emotion as Melinda, taking a short break, walked over and sat down next to her. With a great effort Kendall managed to relax her muscles and to appear outwardly calm, while inside she was seething. Melinda had been given her role in *La Valse,* since she wouldn't have time to learn the part before opening night of their spring season in New York. With her breath suspended, Kendall waited for Melinda to make her usual cutting comment.

"I'm surprise to see you here, Kendall," Melinda whispered, her gaze fastened upon the group of dancers rehearsing their dance.

Kendall's gaze also was trained on the dancers, but her eyes had narrowed. "Why? I am still part of this company."

Melinda twisted about in her chair and looked directly at Kendall. "Yes, you are," she replied slowly, as though it were only a matter of time before that fact changed.

Kendall met Melinda's regard with her own unwavering directness. "And try not to forget that. You may have my role in *La Valse,* but that will be all this season. Enjoy this—victory, if that's what you want to call it, because it will be short-lived."

"Don't be so sure about that." There was a smug tone in Melinda's voice as she stood and readied herself for her entrance. "Just watch Greg and me dance and see how well we perform together."

From years of experience Kendall was able to keep her anger banked, but her stomach churned and her already tattered nerves were frazzled. Even though Melinda was a principal dancer like herself, Kendall's position in the company was more secure. She had her pick of dancing roles with ballets being created for her by Daniel, and Melinda envied that and wanted it for herself.

As Greg and Melinda danced, Kendall's heartbeat slowed to a painful throb. Melinda was right. Greg and she were good together. Watching them working, Kendall realized it had been a mistake to come to the studio. She wasn't emotionally ready to handle a confrontation between Melinda and herself, and the fact that Melinda and Greg were good partners bothered her more than she cared to acknowledge.

However, Kendall forced herself to sit through the rest of the rehearsal. She wouldn't give Melinda the satisfaction of running her off with snide remarks.

When the rehearsal was over, Kendall stood and limped over to Greg. Her partner offered her a bright smile as he wiped his neck and face with a towel.

"I'm glad you came today, Kendall. What do you think of *La Valse*? How do you think Melinda and I look together?"

"You look good. How's the campaign outside the studio going with her?" Kendall schooled her voice to a casual tone. She wouldn't stoop to Melinda's level and cut the dancer down with other members of the company.

"Not bad, and this should help my cause some." Then, as if Greg realized he might have said something wrong, he leaned close to Kendall's ear and whispered, "But you're still the best partner a guy could have. I'll be sorry when Andre returns at the end of the season. I'm going to miss holding you." A teasing grin was plastered all over Greg's face as he placed an arm loosely about Kendall's shoulders and started to walk toward the door.

At the door to the dressing room, Greg turned toward Kendall, running his hand lightly down her cheek, a tenderness in his eyes. "I know what you're going through, Kendall. No one can take your place, though, and I want you to remember that. Now, I think you have a wedding to get ready for." Greg's hand dropped away, the serious expression gone as quickly as it had appeared.

But at the mention of Cara's wedding, a frown tensed Kendall's features. "I wish you hadn't reminded me."

"Cara isn't you. She will have to live her own life and make her own decisions, which might not always coincide with yours."

"Gregory Spencer, you're just full of advice today."

"Once a year I have a day like this." The brilliant smile was back on his face.

"Will I see you at the wedding?" Kendall knew she would need all of her friends around her tonight. She dreaded not only the wedding but also the prospect of seeing Drake again, and paled every time she remembered their last meeting.

"I wouldn't miss this for the world. Besides, there will be another free meal included."

Kendall leaned forward and kissed Greg lightly on his lips.

Surprise widened his eyes. "What was that for?"

"For being you. I'll see you later."

Kendall turned to hobble toward the elevator, but paused for a charged moment when she caught Melinda staring at her, her anger impaling Kendall as if by daggers.

She willed a smile to her lips as she passed Melinda in the hallway. Kendall could feel the other woman's venomous regard on her as she waited for the elevator. Greg might not realize it, but Melinda had laid claim to him and she was going to make sure no other woman got near him. Kendall regretted ever having mentioned Melinda to Greg at Daniel's party, but her only excuse was that she hadn't been herself that evening. Drake had definitely rattled her with his reappearance, and his effect on her hadn't lessened, only intensified until she wasn't sure what to do.

* * *

Kendall and Cara climbed out of the taxi and entered Drake's apartment building, giving their names to the doorman. On the elevator ride up, Cara's hands were nervously twisting together.

"Having second thoughts?" Kendall had noted the touch of paleness in Cara's cheeks.

"Do I look all right?"

"Look all right?" Kendall was surprised by her sister's question. Cara was dressed in a white silk dress that fell to just below her knees in soft folds. The belt, made of the same material as the dress, emphasized Cara's slim waist.

"Do I look like a bride, Kendall? I didn't have much time to find a wedding dress and I decided to buy this so I could also wear it on the plane to Mexico."

"Oh?" For a moment Kendall had hoped that Cara was reconsidering marrying Michael so soon after meeting him. "No, you look great, Cara. White is a good color for you with your dark complexion."

Cara breathed easier. "I want this to be special. I only intend doing this once."

The doors to the elevator opened and across from them was Drake's front door, the solid wood so forbidding. Like the man, Kendall thought as she approached the door, wincing at the pain in her foot, and rang the bell.

Kendall hadn't realized she was holding her breath until her chest began to ache. Slowly she released the trapped air at the same time the door opened to reveal a smiling Drake.

Drake took Cara's hand, saying, "May I kiss the bride now? After the ceremony I doubt I'll be able to get within ten feet of you. You look beautiful, Cara." Drake planted a kiss on Cara's mouth as he drew her into his penthouse.

But when Drake's intense gaze fell on Kendall, the

smile died on his lips, the sparkle in his eyes dimmed. "Hello, Kendall. The guests will be arriving soon, so why don't you two go upstairs to my bedroom and get freshened up for the ceremony? I'll keep Michael out of the way, a feat that's not going to be easy."

The coolness in his eyes didn't diminish as he raked his gaze over Kendall, mentally stripping her with a clinical detachment. Tilting her chin to a defiant angle, she limped toward the stairs with Cara. *He will not get to me,* she vowed silently, but she was having a hard time convincing her heart of the truth of those words.

For a few seconds on the stairs she almost turned and fled from the apartment. Her mind was swamped with memories of that wonderful evening she had spent with Drake here. *Wonderful until the end,* she thought bitterly. He had carried her up these very stairs to his bedroom, where he had proceeded to make love to her with such tenderness that she shivered even now from the memory.

*I don't think I can go upstairs,* she thought, desperation settling over her again. He purposely had placed them in his bedroom to unnerve her, and she fought frantically not to give him the pleasure of seeing her discomfort at his suggestion.

Kendall had turned and had even placed a foot on the last stair behind her when her gaze caught Drake's and his keenly discerning eyes held hers captive. With an iron steadfastness reflected in his gaze, he ascended the stairs toward her. His mouth, which had been set in an unyielding line only moments before, slowly softened into a smile directed totally at her. A current of sensual danger vibrated the air between them as he shortened the distance between them, some new and indefinable tension making her alarmingly aware that they were now alone, Cara having already disappeared upstairs.

Stopping only a stair below her, he didn't try to touch her, but she felt his virile presence in every fiber of her being. He was undermining her firm resolve to forget him and get on with her life. It had only taken one sensuous, thought-destroying look from him to do it, and Kendall couldn't believe what little control she had over her own emotions where he was concerned.

The touches of sunlight returned to his eyes as they wandered over her features. "For this one evening, Kendall, let's try to be civil to one another for Cara and Michael's sakes." His chuckle was low, warm, and arrogant, laced with confidence. "I know it won't be easy, but I'll make an effort."

"You're right about it not being easy. But if we keep our distance maybe we can pull it off." Her desperation had now entered her voice. She had unsuccessfully tried to rekindle her dying anger toward him, but his nearness was doing strange things to her insides, his forceful bearing slowly branding her with his ownership.

He raised one eyebrow mockingly. "Is across the room safe enough for you?" There was amusement in his voice as he deliberately stepped up to stand next to her on the same stair, his hand trailing down her arm, burning her through the cranberry silk material of her dress. "I didn't tell you earlier, Kendall, because I didn't want to take anything away from the bride, but you look beautiful, too. That dress is divine." His scorching gaze traveled leisurely over her face before moving lower until it finally stopped at the V neckline of her dress. "Very lovely," he murmured in a smoky voice meant to seduce her.

His mouth was slowly descending toward hers with

each word he spoke, and Kendall backed away until the balustrade was pressing into her. Placing both arms on either side of her, he effectively trapped her within the cage of his embrace, the corners of his mouth slanting upward.

He lifted one hand and stroked the side of her neck in slow reverence; a wild tremble of excitement jarred her, making her sway toward him. "How have you been, Kendall?"

The huskiness in his voice was eroding all the defenses she had erected before coming to his apartment. She was amazed at how quickly they had crumbled, as though there had been no bitterness between them, as if she had no willpower.

"Fine," she finally answered in a voice that was no more than a whisper, her precarious equilibrium suffering further when his bronzed hand roamed downward, pausing at the V of her neckline. His gaze had followed the progress of his hand, lingering on the quick rise and fall of her breasts.

Then, almost reluctantly, his regard returned to her slightly parted lips, moving slowly upward until it halted at her veiled eyes. His breath mingled with hers, his arms coiling about her to draw her to him. "Are you sure? You're so tense." His hands slid up and down her back in agonizingly slow strokes before he successfully anchored her to his solid frame.

A tremor quaked through her body; her senses flooded with his distinctively male scent that could always cause an increase in the tempo of her heartbeat. Through the fabrics of their clothes Kendall felt the pounding of his heart equaling hers in quickness. For a fleeting moment she reveled in the effect she was having on him. His expression was calm, the only evidence of his arousal the glint in his eyes and his accelerated heartbeat.

"Relax, babe. This is supposed to be a celebration. You're acting as if you're attending a funeral."

His words effectively doused the smoldering embers of her desire, and she tried to struggle free of his embrace. He only tightened his arms about her, molding her completely to his body.

"How can I relax when you're holding me like this?" Her words were spoken through clenched teeth, her eyes pinpoints boring into his amused expression.

"You used to love my holding you—like this." He crushed her even more firmly into him, making it very plain just how aroused he really was.

"Drake, let me go! The key word is *used.*" She renewed her struggle to free herself, her eyes fired with her hostility.

"Afraid?"

She halted and stabbed him with a knifing look. "Yes! Are you satisfied now? Will you leave me alone?"

His intent eyes drilled into her for a static moment; then, without any warning, he ground his mouth into hers with a bruising quickness. Holding her head with his hands, he deepened the kiss, the tongue parting her lips and invading her mouth. Slowly the kiss changed from a show of fierce domination to an infinitely gentle persuasion that tilted Kendall's balance. She found herself clinging to him; her whole body shaking from the force of his desire.

Oh, God, she wished she could hang on to her anger, but he was an expert at stirring her passion.

From afar Kendall heard the doorbell ringing and slowly gathered her spinning senses about her, one part of her wanting whoever was at the door to go away, the other relieved at the interruption.

They drew apart, Drake cursing beneath his breath. "Damn! Couldn't the guests have waited a little longer?" A wry grin slashed across his features. "Like until tomorrow. Oh, well, I guess I'd better start hosting." Unwillingly Drake released her from his embrace and started down the stairs.

Kendall watched him move, his strides smooth and fluid. She felt shaken to her very core. When he had kissed her, her whole dancing career had flashed before her eyes. He exerted too much power over her and she had to escape his masterful control.

Slowly she turned and made her way up the stairs, her hands gripping the balustrade for support, her injured ankle aching. Her legs refused to completely hold her up; her body still trembling from the lingering imprint of his possession.

Cara, pacing around Drake's bedroom, came to a halt when Kendall stepped into the room. For a moment Kendall stood paralyzed just inside the doorway, her gaze riveted upon the brass bed where they had made love. She felt hot and cold at the same time, almost as if she were two distinct people, each warring for control of her emotions. The dancer in her wanted no part of Drake Taylor; the woman wanted him with every ounce of herself.

"Kendall, where have you been?"

Cara's voice sliced through the haze of confusion within Kendall and drew her back to the present. She wrenched her gaze from the bed and looked at her younger sister. "What's wrong?"

Suddenly Cara's tensed features altered, a smile inching

into them. "I guess the prewedding jitters have finally struck me." She held her hands out and they were shaking.

Kendall started to say, "Then don't go through with the marriage," but with a great deal of willpower, which had been lacking only moments before, she resisted the urge. Instead she crossed the room to her sister and took her hands, smiling her reassurances. "I could pounce on that statement but I won't. You've told me enough times in the past to let you live your own life. Well, today I will. I know you don't want me to try and talk you out of marrying Michael. So, all I will tell you is that I hope everything works out for you two. I do like Michael, Cara."

Tears glistened in Cara's eyes. "Oh, Kendall, you don't know how much I needed to hear that from you."

The two sisters fell into each other's arms, tears spilling from Cara's eyes. Giving Cara a comforting hug, Kendall swallowed the lump in her throat and drew back.

"Don't you dare go and spoil that beautiful face." Kendall said with mock sternness.

A wide grin broke through the tears and Cara wiped at them. "No, you're right. I am really happy, Kendall. I know Michael is the man for me."

"How?" The question was spoken before Kendall had realized it.

Cara walked into the bathroom to repair her makeup, saying, "Because I can't imagine my life without him."

The next thirty minutes passed quickly as Kendall and Cara waited in Drake's bedroom for all the guests to arrive. Cara's last words before entering the bathroom played through Kendall's thoughts repeatedly. For the past six years her only salvation had been her dancing. She had been alive then, but what about the rest of the time?

When Drake finally knocked on the bedroom door,

Cara was calm and very eager to get on with the wedding. Kendall couldn't imagine herself being calm, especially faced with the prospects of not dancing for the next two years. What would she do if she couldn't dance? Until Drake had asked her that question, she hadn't thought much about it. But since then she had been constantly asking herself that very question and she wasn't sure of the answer. The inactivity of the past few days was driving her crazy.

"Ladies, if you're ready, the guests are waiting, not to mention one very nervous groom who has been wearing down my patience with his constant questions." Stepping aside, Drake allowed Cara and Kendall to pass him in the doorway. "I know he asked me at least once every five minutes what time it was."

The wedding was a simple one, with Drake standing in as Michael's best man and Kendall as the maid of honor. The forty guests were members of the dance company or colleagues of Michael's at Taylor Industries.

Looking at Cara as she stood next to Michael, exchanging the marriage vows with him, Kendall envied them their love-filled gazes meant only for each other. *What would it feel like to be cherished so lovingly?* Kendall wondered, and glanced away from the couple, a dryness in her throat.

Kendall's attention was drawn to Drake, who was staring at her. The raw impact of his gaze tore the breath from her lungs. Their gazes embraced across the short expanse that separated them, and she drank in the chiseled lines of Drake's face, which was curved in a charming, seductive smile.

Her bones felt as if they were melting under the disarming force of his look. The dancer within her fought her way to the surface, and she jerked her gaze away from the web of sheer sensuality that he was deliberately weaving around her.

After the ceremony and congratulations dinner was served, with several tables set up in Drake's large dining room. Before Kendall realized what Drake was doing, he had captured her elbow and was escorting her into the dining room.

He pulled out a chair and assisted her into it, his breath fanning her neck as he whispered, "It's getting harder to pull that wall up around your emotions, Kendall. One day you're going to stop fighting me and acknowledge you're a woman as well." His words were accompanied by a wickedly rakish grin that underscored his meaning.

Kendall slanted him a withering look, saying in a tight voice, "You're very sure of your—charms. I'm going to take great pleasure in proving you wrong."

His devilish smile grew, encompassing his whole face. "Let's just say I'm very determined where you're concerned, babe."

"Stop calling me that!" Her voice had risen above a whisper, drawing stares from the people around them. In a more controlled voice, Kendall continued, "I want nothing from you, Drake Taylor."

Laughter burst forth in the dark depths of his eyes, black with his desire. "Tell that to your traitorous body, my dear."

"Oh!" Kendall pointedly looked away from Drake and somehow managed to divert her attention from him all through the dinner. But her traitorous body felt his presence, as if it were a commanding, aggressive force mesmerizing her every sense. The hour she'd had to sit next to him had been one of her hardest travails in a long time, worse even than her first audition for the Manhattan Ballet Company.

Fortunately Daniel monopolized Drake's attention as everyone was standing and leaving the dining room. It afforded Kendall the time needed to escape his company without his stopping her. Safely seated on a couch in the living room with Drake across the room from her, Kendall relaxed, her ankle throbbing from all the walking and standing she had done all day. Leaning back and making herself more comfortable, she watched the guests dance to a small combo that Drake had hired to play.

Obviously he hadn't spared any expense, Kendall thought, remembering the delicious lobster and steak dinner. Probably, though, he felt guilty for sending Michael to Alaska. But in the back of Kendall's mind she wondered if Drake would feel guilty about anything.

The minutes inched into an hour. Now that she had kissed Cara and Michael good-bye, wishing them a wonderful honeymoon trip to Mexico, she was ready to leave also. But most of guests were still dancing and drinking, and Kendall felt since her sister had left that she should at least stay awhile longer.

It wasn't that she was bored, since she enjoyed talking with her fellow dancers about the ballet, which was usually their main topic of conversation. But every time Kendall looked up, her gaze would collide with Drake's. Even across the width of his large living room, the magnetic strength of his personality coiled about her, threatening to suffocate her. The bold recklessness in his penetrating regard sharpened her awareness of him.

"Kendall, have you heard one word of what I'm saying?" Greg's amused voice pierced the hypnotic spell that Drake's look had woven, and she snapped her attention back to her partner, who was sitting next to her on the couch.

"No. I'm sorry, Greg. What were you saying?"

"Never mind what I was saying. What's going on with you and him?" Greg stressed the word *him*, his eyes darting to the subject under discussion.

"Nothing."

"Bull! Kendall, I wasn't born yesterday and I do have two good eyes."

"And you're the company gossip." Humor spiced her quick retort. "Ah, I see Melinda, and I don't think she's too happy that you're spending time with me."

"Kendall, you may think I'm the company gossip, which, by the way, I am not, but I'm also your friend. Something has definitely been wrong since that party at Daniel's. If you ever need a friend to talk to, think about me." Greg held up one of his hands, palm toward Kendall. "Scout's honor I won't breathe a word of it to another soul."

"Gregory Spencer, I doubt seriously you were ever a Boy Scout, but thanks anyway." Her blue eyes warmed under the look of friendship in Greg's.

"Greg, I think it's time we leave. We have a long day of rehearsals tomorrow for *La Valse.*" Melinda's voice was coated with acid, her sharp words directed more at Kendall than at Greg. "I know some people don't have to worry about getting up early as we do."

The light in Greg's eyes diminished slightly as he stared up at Melinda towering over them. "If you're that worried about your sleep, then I suggest you call a taxi."

Melinda's eyes grew round, a gasp escaping her lips. "Greg, I thought . . ."

"You owned me. No, my dear, you don't."

Fury leaped to life in Melinda's cat eyes, and before a scene could develop, Kendall quickly interjected, "Greg, I'll see you later at the studio. I might be in tomorrow."

Seeing Melinda's beautiful features marred with a frown, Greg thought it was wise to take Melinda home before all hell broke loose. He enjoyed Melinda's company, but at times she could be too possessive. He also knew of Melinda's ambition to take Kendall's place in the company. Kendall could look after herself, but it wouldn't be easy with someone like Melinda, who could fight dirty. He would have to keep an eye on her.

Greg tossed Kendall a sheepish grin before standing and guiding Melinda away. Kendall inhaled deeply, not aware of Melinda's effect on her until the dancer had gone. Kendall's hands were clenched so tightly in her lap that her fingernails had stabbed her palms.

Just as Kendall relaxed, a deep, rich voice said, "I was going to give Spencer one more minute, then I was going to commit a breach of etiquette. One does not bodily eject an invited guest." Drake folded his long length beside her, amusement glittering in his eyes.

Kendall stiffened, the tensing movement sharply reminding her of her injury. "But then, you never did go by the rules."

Laughter rumbled in his chest. "You know me well, Kendall."

Drake had completely dissolved the space between them. He went on casually discussing the wedding, the weather, the New York Yankees. He was being too nice, Kendall thought, dragging a shaky hand through her hair, the gesture conveying the tension that was twisting around inside her.

Then suddenly his voice fell, his tone becoming intimate. "I'll drive you home, Kendall, after everyone has left."

"No! I'll call a taxi."

He smiled angelically, a roguish gleam winking deep in his eyes as he made an assessing sweep of her features. "I promise I will take you straight home—if that is what you want. But I have something I need to discuss with you."

"What?"

"Stick around and find out." Drake rose in one fluid motion and walked away from her, his lithe strides underscoring his self-assurance.

## *CHAPTER SEVEN*

The penthouse was quiet for the first time in hours, but the silence wasn't a welcome sound to Kendall. Drake closed the door on the last wedding guest and slowly turned toward her, his expression unreadable.

Suddenly she questioned the wisdom of staying after the other guests had left. She must be going crazy from the past few days' inactivity if she had allowed him to talk her into this! But Drake knew her better than she would like to admit. He had challenged her and he knew she wouldn't refuse a challenge. That was one of the reasons why she danced. It was a constant challenge to do better, to become perfect.

"If I remember correctly, you like white wine."

The richness of his voice centered her full attention on Drake, standing in front of her with a glass of wine in one hand. She reached up and took the glass from him, the brief collision with his fingers eroding her self-control even more. Taking several sips of her wine, she severed eye contact with him, and instead stared toward the terrace and the black of night beyond.

He sat down next to her and every muscle in her body tensed. It was becoming increasingly hard for her to deny his surging magnetism; it was enveloping her, absorbing her.

"Relax, Kendall." He chuckled softly as his arm slid about her shoulders and pulled her back against the couch and him, his hand stroking her, commanding her to yield.

She resisted the magic of his fingers and placed a few inches between them, twisting about to face him squarely. "You had something to discuss with me." Her voice was amazingly level, considering that she could hardly think straight with his eyes sensuously scanning her features.

"I'm going to Grand Lake this weekend and I want you to come with me."

His words sent shock waves coursing through her. "Go with you!"

The laugh lines at the corners of his eyes crinkled, his eyes glowing with a dark gleam. "Hear me out first before you start berating me." Humor was sprinkled through his words as he reduced the space between them, taking her hands in his.

Kendall could feel his uneasiness in the touch of his hands. He wasn't as calm and relaxed as he wanted her to think. A coiled tension snaked about them, linking them together.

"Six years ago you didn't give our relationship a chance to work. You walked out before it could. Now I want to find out if it can work."

"No!" Kendall tried to yank her hands from his, but his grip imprisoned them.

"You owe me, Kendall. You took the coward's way out then and left me angry, frustrated, and wondering if we could have made it. For six years I've felt a part of my life has been unresolved. I grant you, we may not have a chance, but if you're truthful with yourself you will admit that things aren't completely over between us."

His thumb massaged the back of her hand in slow lazy movements, but his alert eyes were gauging the minute changes in her expression. Behind his smile his inner tension was building as he waited for her response.

The woman part of her wanted to go desperately, to believe they had a chance, but the dancer in her cautioned her about getting involved with a man whom she knew could hurt her badly. Was he setting her up to avenge himself for what she had done six years ago? That question nagged at her as indecision warred within.

"Drake, I—"

Both of his hands clasped her head, his look silencing the words of refusal. Slowly, almost hesitantly, his mouth lowered onto hers, the kiss deepening and softening at the same time. The depth of his passion was transmitted in the tremor of his hands that held her head still.

Was it possible there was no revenge tied up in this? Was it possible that she needed something other than her dancing to fulfill her? Those questions would never be answered if she didn't accept his invitation.

His mouth left hers to trail feather-light kisses down her neck, his arms slipping around to gather her to him. Her arms went around him as he nibbled on her earlobe, a place he knew excited her. Her body again acknowledged the power this man had over her senses even as her mind fought against it.

She had to think away from him. With him so near, any decision would be colored. Parting from him slightly, Kendall looked deeply into the swirling passion of his eyes.

"Drake, I need some time to think—alone."

"I'm leaving tomorrow afternoon."

Completely cutting her ties with Drake, she stood, saying, "Then I'll call you by twelve."

Rising, he faced her, his heavily veiled look concealing his expression. "Don't deny the part of you that wants to say yes. For once, let go of your emotions and just feel." There was a quiet steel in his words that underlined his meaning.

"I'm not sure I can. I've always had to be so strong and in control from an early age that the only place I've been able to let go is in my dancing."

"And when you no longer have your dancing, how will you express those emotions?"

Again that plaguing question! "I don't know."

He lifted his hand to stroke her cheek, the touch a combination of tenderness and roughness, much like the man. "Learn to give of yourself. Learn to trust another person with your feelings."

"I live in a world that is dominated by one thing—dancing. There hasn't been room for much else."

"Then, don't you think it's time to make room?" His hand cupped her nape and pulled her to him, his mouth settling over hers in a gentle exploration. When he drew away, his hand dropped to his side and he turned toward the front door. "I'd better take you home now." His voice was edged with emotion.

The ride to her apartment was made in silence, Kendall's attention directed out the window at the streets of New York. People were everywhere, even this late at night. The city never slept.

At her apartment Drake took Kendall's key and unlocked her front door. Then, with their gazes locking, they stood in the deserted hallway, each trying to read the other's expression. Finally Drake leaned forward and brushed his lips across hers before turning and walking away without a word.

Inside her apartment Kendall sank down onto her couch, propping her aching leg up on the coffee table, the darkness like a comforting sheath. If she turned the lights on, she would have to acknowledge the emptiness of the apartment and she wasn't ready to. With Cara on her honeymoon, the loneliness of the past week would be heightened.

Conflicting emotions raged inside her; her head throbbed with indecision. If she accepted his invitation she could end up being hurt. *But,* her weary mind reasoned, *at least you will be feeling.* As the clock ticked away the minutes, an intense feeling of loneliness revolved about her, compelling her to make the only decision she knew in her heart was right.

Before she could change her mind, she reached for the phone and dialed Drake's apartment. It was nearly four in the morning, but when Drake answered, his voice was alert, as though he had been waiting for her call.

"What's the weather like in Oklahoma?" Kendall asked to diffuse the mounting tension within herself.

He laughed, the sound rich and warm. "Unusually balmy for this time of year. But then, you know how quickly that can change in Oklahoma."

"Then I'll pack for all types of weather."

When Drake's Learjet landed at Tulsa International, the tension within Kendall knotted in her stomach and fingered outward. It was six years since she had last been in her hometown. The memories assailed her, twisting deep into her mind and bringing forth all the pain and joy of that final year in Tulsa.

As if he sensed what she was thinking, Drake's arm stole about her waist and cradled her to him as they exited the plane and walked toward a waiting car. Jumbled sensations were flooding her, shimmering waves of passion mixed with her fear of what lay ahead for her and Drake. An uncertain future stretched before them like the highway that was taking them to Drake's cabin on Grand Lake of the Cherokees northeast of Tulsa.

As they neared the cabin, Kendall again questioned her wisdom in coming. This was where it had all begun for them. Would their relationship end here or begin again? she wondered as Drake brought the car to a stop before the "cabin," a four-bedroom house situated on a bluff overlooking the lake, water on three sides of his property.

Drake had said nothing during the journey from Tulsa, as though he respected her need to grow accustomed to the feelings overwhelming her. But now he speared her with an absorbing concentration and said, "For one weekend I want you to forget that there's another world out there. Don't run from your feelings and don't shut me out."

There was a quiet plea in his voice, a glimpse of vulnerability, that unnerved her, telegraphing the hurt that she had caused him six years before when she had walked away without facing him with her inner feelings and doubts. But at twenty she had been young, innocent, and afraid of what he could provoke in her. The fear was still there, but it was coupled with a need to experience a complete fulfillment that she was quickly realizing not even her dancing had brought her.

Kendall swallowed away the tightness in her throat and

searched for the right words to say. For an electrified moment the air crackled with their raw emotions.

"I'll try, Drake. That's all I can promise." She wanted to say more, but the words *I love you* wouldn't come forth. The feeling was there, but years of experience at keeping her emotions bottled up inside kept her from saying what was in her heart.

Drake framed her face with his powerful hands. His unwavering regard, packed with sensuality, was creating a net of arousal thread by thread as it sought what was in her heart. "Thank you, Kendall."

Her brow creased in a question. "For what?"

"For coming this weekend. For giving us the chance I think we deserve."

An intoxication was assailing her lungs; each breath she dragged into her was not quite enough. "That's not what you felt a month ago."

"That feeling was there underneath the anger." The arrogant slant of his mouth slashed upward.

"Is the anger still there?"

"Probably. Something that has been with you for years won't vanish overnight." His growing smile softened the implication of his words.

"I'm sorry about how I handled things then. Running away, I can see now, wasn't the right answer."

"When I met you, I thought I'd found what I had been subconsciously looking for all my adult years. I never intended to be a confirmed bachelor. I—"

Kendall placed a finger over his firm, sensual lips, silencing words that she felt could destroy the tentative truce that had been declared between them. Already his smile had dimmed, a tenseness evident in his hands on her face.

"There is no tomorrow and no yesterday. Only today, Drake." Her eyes silently implored him to halt his sojourn into the past before anger should stand between them again.

For a taut moment Drake said nothing; then he grinned, warm currents swirling in the brown depths of his eyes. "Come on. Let's leave our luggage in the car and go for a walk."

Drake had slid from the car and was helping Kendall out. He folded her tightly and tenderly to him, his lips joining with hers. Her mouth yielded to the heated challenge of his and returned her own.

"I want you all to myself for four days. I'm taking the phone off the hook and I refuse to answer the front door. Woman, you are stuck with me," he muttered into her ear.

The twin assault of his breath on her neck and his hands drawing patterns of delight over her back were shocking her senses with the overwhelming intensity of the passion that had lain dormant in him for six years.

"Can we walk along the bluff now?" Kendall murmured, pulling away to gaze up into his face.

The sun was beginning to set and they often had walked to the bluff's edge to look at the sunset over the lake. He remembered, too, the feelings of oneness and closeness they had experienced when they had quietly stared out over the water. The memory of their intimacy was mirrored in his eyes, the golden sparks in his dark eyes flaming at the thought.

His arm fitted about her waist and they began strolling toward the lake, the heat of an unusually warm day lingering with them. At the edge of the small bluff Kendall sucked in her breath sharply at the beauty before her. The western sky was a rainbow of purples, reds, pinks, boldly fanning outward from the sinking sun. The sunset was reflected in the lake, glimmering like liquid fire in the water beyond them.

Wordlessly they stood on the bluff while each absorbed the beauty of the dying day and became lost in the memory of a yesterday. It would make matters much simpler if they could forget what had taken place between them six years before, but Kendall now realized the impossibility of that—not when they had traveled back in time to a place where they had shared a lot of deep, intense feelings. The past was all around them at the cabin, and Kendall suddenly decided they had to meet it head-on and clear up what had happened then.

"Drake," she said, tentatively breaking the companionable silence between them, "we need to talk."

"I know. I felt it, too." There was a gentle smile in his words, in his warm expression as he turned toward her and clasped her upper arms.

Her heartbeat was no longer steady, rhythmic like the waves lapping the shore below them. Instead it slammed against her chest at the disarming look Drake was sending her. She was mesmerized, held immobile beneath the fiery splendor that flared to life in his eyes. His scent drugged her senses, her own spiraling passion written on her features.

"But not now, babe. Talk is the farthest thing from my mind when you look at me like that."

His words produced a tightly aching dryness in her throat and mouth. Slowly her tongue licked her lips to moisten them as she tried to restore some semblance of rationality to her chaotic thoughts, but the effort was useless. Her body was demanding his total possession.

Sensing her powerful need, Drake swept Kendall up into his arms and headed back toward the house. But they never reached the cabin. Instead Drake took her to an enclosed, white pavilion, situated halfway up the slope to the house, and gently deposited her on the couch. His look, when he stood again at his full height, was worshipful; the need to talk with words was gone.

Kneeling down, he slowly began to unbutton her shirt, the slight trembling of his hands indicating the intensity of his arousal. The cotton material fell apart to expose her breasts to his adoring gaze. With brushing strokes, he circled each one, then bent forward and took a taut nipple into his mouth, sucking gently, lightly nipping at it.

"Oh, Drake," Kendall moaned, burying her fingers in the toasty brown waves of his hair.

He looked up to pin her beneath his smoldering warmth for an endless moment before returning his full attention to the other rosy tip. Then in maddeningly slow motion he proceeded to remove her shirt, first down one arm then the other.

When his hand went to the zipper on her slacks, her sharply indrawn breath spoke of the exquisite desire bolting through her in delightful anticipation of what was to come. Again as if he had all the time in the world, he leisurely drew her slacks down her legs, his hands lingering on the tingling flesh of her inner thighs.

When he stroked her, Kendall caught a glimpse of a crack in his carefully controlled passion. For the moment he had a tight leash on his emotions, wanting to bring her pleasure above his own needs and desire. The warm contentment she felt at this new insight into him propelled her to sit up, wanting only to give of herself as he had.

"Now it's my turn to undress you, Drake."

Kendall stood, clad only in her lace panties, and tugged his silk shirt out of his black pants. With deliberately slow movements she teased him as he had teased her, one torturous button at a time. Then she slid her hands over his hair-roughened chest with insolent touches that elicited a deep moan from him, his body quaking beneath her fingertips.

His large tanned hands covered hers, halting their suggestive strokes. "No more," he rasped, his breathing labored, his eyes glazed with passion.

"Oh, no, Drake Taylor. I'm not finished with you. If you can dish it out, then you can certainly take it," she taunted him.

His brown eyes, slumberous with desire, narrowed slightly, but his hands dropped away. Even so, his breathing was shallow, the rapturous look deepening in his eyes as Kendall continued her sweet torment. Sliding his zipper down, she pushed his pants along his long, sinewy legs, her fingernails tantalizing his thighs with light scratches, further inciting him.

When his black pants lay on the floor next to his shirt and Kendall's clothing, he gently shoved her back onto the couch, saying in a grating voice as he hastily removed his last garment, "That's it. For six years I've dreamed about you. Once you got into my system I found it near impossible to rid myself of you."

He quickly slipped her panties from her and tossed them across the room. Then he stretched his muscular length along her slender frame and pulled her into his embrace, branding her with the fire of his sensual tension. His tongue mingled with the eagerness of hers while his hand toyed with a hardened nipple, his palm kneading her sensitive surfaces.

As his poignant search of her mouth deepened, her hands explored the hard planes of his body. Trapped in a building passion that was quickly becoming unbearable, Drake sought to unleash it. Without any subtlety he parted her legs with his knee, his body poised above hers; then he lowered himself onto her.

As he filled her with himself, shudder after shudder of excitement passed through him and into her like a bolt of electricity. At the peak of their completion, she cried out his name, her fingernails scraping over the hard muscles of his back.

Afterward they lay entwined in each other's arms and legs, a heated pleasure radiating to every part of her, warming her even though the air was becoming chilly in the enclosed pavilion with the descent of night. She would treasure this moment forever. She now accepted the fact that they had become lovers again. There would be no running away this time, for she realized she did owe their relationship a chance.

"We still need to talk, Drake."

A tensing of his body was transmitted along hers, his arms tightening their hold. "Yes, but not now. The time is not right."

They fell into a thoughtful silence as they both gathered their fragile emotions together. What they had just shared had been so special that she knew Drake was afraid, as she was, of what had to be said. For the moment, though, Kendall decided to relish the oneness that existed between them and not to worry about the future. They would talk later.

The dark shadows of night had completely cloaked the

landscape when Drake and Kendall walked hand and hand up to the car and retrieved their luggage. Inside the cabin Kendall took a moment to acclimate herself to the once familiar surroundings of Drake's place on the lake.

Nothing had changed and yet so much had. The furniture consisted of the same modern pieces as before; the dominant colors navy blue and white with splashes of lime green. Everything was in its right place, the cabin immaculately clean, but the house appeared as though no one had lived in it for a long time.

"When was the last time you came here, Drake?" Kendall was almost afraid to ask the question, for she sensed what the answer would be before he replied.

"This is the second time since you left. The first was right after you went to New York, but I only stayed an hour. Too much had happened between us here. Too many memories, Kendall." His voice was faintly rough, faintly gritty. "Once I thought of selling it, but I couldn't bring myself to put it on the market."

Kendall again recalled all the special times they had spent at the cabin; their first meeting, the time she had finally broken down and wept after her mother's death, the first time they had made love, and finally the day Drake had asked her to marry him.

She hadn't realized until his admission that her leaving had affected him so intensely. Those last few weeks they had been together they had argued a lot, mainly about her dancing and his job that would take him to Saudi Arabia. She had thought then that they were going in opposite directions with no common ground between them and that she should sever their connection quickly and cleanly. Had she been mistaken?

"I didn't realize," Kendall finally whispered. Her gaze fastened on Drake's back; his hands were jammed into his pants pockets as he stared out the picture window at the lake.

"I've never been very good at opening up to another person, Kendall. You didn't realize because I didn't tell you how deeply I felt."

Her hands trembled as she reached out and touched him, and her voice quavered as she asked, "And how do you feel now?"

"The truth is, I don't know anymore. I started out seeing you again to make you pay for the hurt that had been eating away at me. Now I just don't know." His shoulders sagged under the weight of her hands.

Kendall slid her arms around him and laid her head on his back. "It seems we both have a lot to work out. We have changed. Six years has made us different, Drake. But I think this weekend at your cabin is a good place for us to begin finding some answers."

Drake turned within the circle of her arms. "I want all of you, Kendall, not just pieces of your life here and there. Are you ready for that? Can you devote as much energy to me as you do to your dancing?"

"I can offer no guarantees, Drake. I only know that when we make love, the feelings I experience are unique. Not even my dancing can make me the complete woman that I am in your arms."

The smile that stole into his features was incredibly tender, the sparkle in his eyes illuminating a possessive warmth. "That's not a bad beginning." He bent forward and brushed her lips with light kisses. "I'm starved. Who's going to fix dinner?"

A soft laugh rolled from Kendall's throat. "Have you forgotten what a lousy cook I am?"

"Actually, no. I was just hoping that you had managed to learn a few things in six years."

With merriment dancing in her eyes, she shook her head. "Thank goodness Cara learned how."

Drake disengaged himself from her and headed for the kitchen. "You're just lucky, woman, that I know how to cook, or we would be two very hungry people before the weekend was through." At the doorway into the kitchen he glanced back with silent laughter edging his features. "You can manage to tear up some lettuce for the salad, can't you?"

She shot him a lancing look that only caused him to toss back his head and openly laugh. Seething, she marched past him into the kitchen, determined to make the best salad possible. All her life she had concentrated on one thing, her dancing, leaving the mundane chores for someone else to do, and cooking had been one of them.

But as she shared the kitchen with Drake she began to reassess her idea that cooking was merely a chore. The light bantering between them sent a contentment flowing over her that she hadn't thought possible with Drake a month before. He patiently showed her how to make a special sauce for the steaks he was grilling outside and then he watched carefully as she mixed up a buttermilk salad dressing.

When they sat down for dinner in front of the picture window, with the moonlight and two candles on the table as their only light, the contented feeling within Kendall was strengthened even more. Kendall floated through the cleanup chores, the looks Drake was telegraphing her making her feel as though she were the center of the universe, the most beautiful woman in the world. In his eyes she saw his desire for her, but also something much deeper: his love.

## *CHAPTER EIGHT*

Kendall sat on the redwood bench on Drake's balcony with her knees drawn up to her chest and her head resting on them. She stared across the lawn toward the lake where the sun was blazing a path upward, the eastern horizon aflame with reds and oranges.

When she had awakened a short while before, the gray shadows of predawn were clinging to the corners of Drake's bedroom. In the dim light she boldly inspected Drake's features, shrouded in the calmness of a deep sleep.

During the three days they had been at the cabin, she had often wanted to look at him with the love she felt deep inside of herself, but always something had held her back. Words of love hadn't been spoken once since they had arrived. She thought Drake still loved her, that what they had shared six years before hadn't diminished, but instead had intensified. Doubts, though, always lingered in the dark recesses of her mind and she masked her true feelings from him. Only when they made love did she let herself express those feelings while each was caught up in the wildly passionate moment.

This is our last day here, she thought with a heavy sigh. She had to go back to New York and start working out again before she lost another role to Melinda, but still she hated the idea of leaving.

The yellow-orange sun was beginning to warm the chill of an early spring day. Kendall straightened to roll her head, easing the tension in her neck that the thought of leaving had produced. That brought to mind the time two days before when Drake had insisted on massaging her. Shivers streaked through her when she recalled how that massage had ended.

During the weekend they had played, relaxed, and laughed, discovering new things about each other. Every day Drake had taken her sailing; then at night they had strolled along the bluff under a shimmering sky before fixing dinner and eating before the fireplace. When they had retired for the night, they had made love with a fierce abandon, each belonging to the other, clinging together as if they were holding each other for the last time.

Kendall felt as though she had become a part of Drake. When she thought of herself, she now thought of Drake, too, as though they had become inseparable. And when they talked of the future into the late hours of each night, Drake talked as if they would be together. At the cabin they were in their own small world where nothing existed but themselves, and Kendall was reluctant to leave that world. What would happen when they both returned to New York and their demanding careers? Would another barrier fall into place between them? Kendall was afraid of the answers to those questions.

Strong, muscular arms snaked about her and hauled her back against a rock-hard chest. A slow, lazy smile moved across Kendall's features as she inhaled deeply of Drake's scent.

Nuzzling her neck, he whispered, "I missed you when

I awakened, babe." His teeth nibbled a path of pure delight from her earlobe down her neck, tingles stirring, unfolding, and curling through her.

"You were sleeping so soundly that I didn't have the heart to wake you." Kendall twisted about in his arms, their mouths only inches apart.

"Babe, I give you permission to wake me anytime you want. Believe me, I won't mind." Drake dragged her to her feet, a devilish grin on his face. "Now, woman, I'm hungry—and for food. I really worked up an appetite last night. And if I remember correctly, you promised me yesterday that you would fix me breakfast in bed today."

"But you're already dressed," Kendall protested. Laughter, like the sun glistening off Grand Lake, brightened her blue eyes as her gaze drank in his powerfully proportioned body clad in tight-fitting jeans and a black pullover sweater.

"Excuses. Excuses. Are you going to back out on a promise?"

"Made under duress. You were tickling me and threatening to throw me overboard into the freezing water."

They had been out sailing and had anchored in the middle of a cove to eat a picnic lunch. One thing had led to another and before Kendall had realized it, they were playfully wrestling. Of course, she was the loser, with Drake pinning her beneath him on the deck.

"A teacher must test his pupil," Drake murmured, humor filtering into his eyes.

While preparing every meal Drake had painstakingly given her cooking lessons, but Kendall had a mental block against cooking. In school she had always loved to sew but had hated to cook.

Stepping away from him, she started for the sliding

glass door, tossing over her shoulder with a teasing grin, "Which means the teacher will have to eat everything the pupil makes."

Laughter rang deep in his chest, the sound permeating the silence of a new day with a radiating glow that matched the sun's. "I think I'm going to regret dragging that promise from you."

"You bet, Drake Taylor. I'm not ready for my solo flight, but you're going to get one huge breakfast, so get into bed."

Kendall had every intention of making him a wonderful breakfast fit for a man who had a large appetite. But somehow by the time she had laid the plate on the tray to carry in to Drake, the breakfast consisted of burnt toast—the third try—strong coffee that she was afraid the spoon would dissolve in it if she stirred it, and two fried eggs with broken yolks.

Sheepishly Kendall placed the tray on Drake's lap and turned quickly to leave, embarrassed at her poor attempt. She had always rallied to a challenge and met it head on, usually doing a good job. But not this time.

Drake seized her wrist and pulled her back down onto the bed, his face void of expression. "Why don't you join me for breakfast?" His eyes scanned the mess before him. "This looks—interesting."

"That's not quite what I would call it. But, no thanks. I'm not hungry."

Quickly, though, Kendall's embarrassment faded. It was hard for her to contain her laughter as Drake suffered through the breakfast, wincing when he took his first sip of the bitter coffee. He lavished cherry jam on his burnt toast, but even that didn't mask the charred flavor.

When he was through, he removed the tray to the table

next to the bed, saying, "Not bad for the first time out. You'll do better next time."

"What are you, a masochist?" Her eyebrows quirked upward in the face of his cheerful, optimistic observation.

"No. Just a man in love with a wonderful, very human woman."

His gaze trapped hers and her heart began to hammer madly. Golden flames of rekindled desire shimmered in his eyes. He brushed his fingertips over her lips, outlining her mouth with sensual slowness.

"You know, Kendall Sinclair Lawrence, that I love you very much and want to marry you. Six years hasn't changed that. Will you marry me?"

His question had robbed her of her voice, her will to think about anything but him and his commanding power. For long moments all she could do was stare into his brown eyes, the two golden lights in them growing, threatening to suck her into the bottomless pool of his ardor.

He gripped her upper arms, mistaking her silence for a denial. "Kendall, I won't ask you to give up your dancing. I'm not forcing you to make a choice. Your dancing is you, but I do want to share in your life completely and totally. Living together, having an affair, isn't the answer. I want a commitment from you."

Kendall finally surfaced from her dazed state and threw her arms around his neck. "Yes, Drake. Yes, I'll marry you." Each word was punctuated with a light but burning kiss.

Drake drew back slightly to look deeply into her eyes. "You mean that?"

She nodded.

"I want us to get married right away. Today."

"I'm not going to back out this time, Drake." This time

she would marry him and any problems they had they would work out together. She wasn't going to run away because she knew she would never love anyone as she did Drake.

"I know. But I can't wait. I've waited for six years. That's the extent of my patience, babe."

Drake threw back the sheet to reveal that he had undressed but had forgotten to don his pajama bottoms. A roguish glint captured his eyes as a sexy smile slid across his mouth.

"I haven't properly thanked you for the breakfast." Drake wound one arm around her and tugged her to him.

Kendall stood at the sliding glass doors that led to Drake's terrace off his bedroom at the penthouse. In the distance she saw Central Park, the lights of New York at nighttime. Drake's arms encased her in a velvet cocoon, his breath whispering against her neck.

"Well, Mrs. Taylor, how does it feel to be married"—he lifted his arm and looked at his watch—"six hours and twenty minutes?"

"I'm not sure, Mr. Taylor. Everything has been so hectic. I'll have to think on that one." She angled her head as if she were in deep thought.

Drake, though, could see her smile in the reflection of the glass doors, and decided to exact a payment for that teasing statement. He whirled her around to face him and immediately crushed his lips into hers. If he hadn't been holding her head, she would have fallen backward from the fierce hunger of his kiss. Seconds became minutes and the kiss lengthened with a primitive urgency that stunned Kendall's dizzying senses.

With the grinding pressure of his mouth still fastened

to hers, each breath was difficult. But Kendall didn't care, for her desire had leaped instantly to a raging inferno at the first contact with him. The wildfire chased through her body, totally out of control.

When he raised his head and looked deeply into her eyes, his face wore an expression of intense longing. He brought her left hand to his lips and kissed each fingertip, lingering on her third finger, where there was a single wide golden band. "I've wanted this for a long time, my wife. I need you by my side. I ache for you." His voice had roughened to a low vibrancy that sent quivering sensations through her at lightning speed.

She wanted, too, when Drake swept her into his arms and carried her to the brass bed, gently settling her on his velour coverlet, his gaze devouring her passion-filled features. She needed, too, when he slowly removed each of her garments, as if he were worshiping her with his hands and eyes, drawing out each touch until he felt her quaking reaction. She yearned, too, when he fitted his magnificent body, stripped of his clothing, next to hers and murmured words of love into her ear, the wooing timbre of his voice reflecting his own heightened desire as his fingers grazed a tingling path over her highly sensitive skin, his lips following suit. She ached, too, when he teased her with his breathy kisses that never quite claimed her lips, only promising wickedly sinful delights.

With each touch he drew her further into the dazzling realm of passionate expression where his caresses were exquisitely sensuous and excitingly heady, overpowering her with their branding possession. With each kiss she longed for more, crying out with her arching body for his final, ultimate link with her.

He praised her. He seduced her. He loved her with each

gentle touch of his hands on her face, throat, breasts, thighs, until she could bear no more.

"Please, Drake, now!"

He took her head within his hands and captured her attention, the firelight in his eyes matching the radiance of hers. All the love he felt for her was mirrored in his face as he stared down at her for a long moment, as though he couldn't quite believe she was here in his bed, his wife.

Then, slowly, with their eyes still embracing, he joined with her and quickly whisked her into another universe for lovers only, where everything within them converged on one incredibly ecstatic moment in time, suspended, savored, held.

Later, lying next to Drake, Kendall marveled at how fully Drake had made her aware of herself, her beauty, her femininity. Until he had entered her life for the second time, she had thought of herself only as a dancer. But he was changing that and one part of Kendall was fighting against the change. She still at times grasped desperately at the old, the familiar.

"I love you, Kendall," Drake whispered into the quiet of the moment, his indisputable maleness displayed in his voice.

Drake was a man of contradictions. He could be rough and tender at the same time. He could be so strong and formidable, but also kind and caring. His understanding was bound up in his self-assurance and sensitivity. But there had been times when he had been extremely possessive, unyielding. And his strength and gentleness were exhibited in his lovemaking, making her feel totally loved, completely desired, and absolutely possessed. Those feelings were new to her. Before in their past, she had glimpsed the depth of emotions between them but had never fully experienced them.

Kendall nestled closer to Drake, a warm rapture flowing over her. "I love you very much, my darling," she murmured against his sweat-dampened chest.

The silence reigned again and slowly Kendall drifted into a contented, deep sleep where she became the Firebird trapped by the prince, Drake, and held captive. A restlessness entered her contented sleep and stayed with her when she awakened the following morning. She told herself she was being ridiculous and finally she was able to banish the unsure feelings her dream had produced.

For a long time Kendall lay in bed, relishing the warmth of the sun as it blanketed her face, Drake's scent clinging to his pillow, the memories of the night before. Earlier she had felt a light kiss on her love-swollen lips and that had aroused her from her sleep. Now she wondered where Drake was.

As she was about to thrust back the sheets and seek him out, Drake strolled into their bedroom with a tray in his hands, humming a light tune. "One good deed deserves another," he said in response to the round look of surprise in her eyes.

"I'm almost afraid to look, then," she answered with a laugh, remembering the breakfast she had served him the day before.

"I was sorely tempted to make you as wonderful a meal as you made me, but what I have in mind for the next week will require a lot of strength, my love." Drake's eyes twinkled with a devilish gleam that prompted Kendall's heartbeat to increase its tempo.

"And just what do you have in mind, sir?" Bending forward, Kendall smelled the single perfect yellow rose that was in a bud vase on the tray, the sweet fragrance mingling with Drake's.

His masculinity was beginning to work on her as he sat down next to her and began to share the breakfast he had made for them. She couldn't seem to get enough of him!

"A honeymoon in Hawaii. I've already called the office and told them I won't be in until next week. Work be damned." Drake's deft fingers tore a piece of toast in half and he took a bite.

"I can't go on a honeymoon right now, Drake."

Kendall felt the taut ribbon that was quickly pulled through his body and realized it was time for the "talk" that they had delayed perhaps far too long. She closed her eyes for a moment to assemble herself, his nearness making that feat very difficult.

"Why not?" The question was spoken low, with lethal quiet.

"Because I'm going to start working out tomorrow. My ankle feels good and I can't miss any more classes or rehearsals. My injury has already caused me to lose one important role. I won't allow another part to go to someone else." Kendall's mind produced a smug-faced Melinda on its screen and Kendall's decision was vehemently strengthened.

"Surely a few days or a week won't make much difference."

The steel thread in his voice tightened a band around Kendall's chest and she fought to drag air into her lungs. They had only been married one day and they were already at odds. She had to stand up for her career now or he would never understand. She had to make him see what it meant to her.

"Every day a dancer is away from dancing, it takes that

much longer for her to get back into dancing shape. I can't afford to go on a honeymoon until after the spring season is over in June."

"I see. Your dancing career is more important than a honeymoon." He rose slowly to tower over her, spearing her with a contemptuous look. "It didn't take long for you to draw the lines in our marriage."

Kendall carefully placed the tray to one side and stood, too, not wanting Drake to have such a height advantage. She met the angry impact of his stare with an uncompromising resolve. "Why are you pressing the issue? We'll go on a honeymoon in a few months."

"Because for once I want you to put me before your damn dancing. Because I think it's important to our marriage to get to know each other well in order to weather the difficult times. A honeymoon gives us that time to be alone, away from outside influences, to strengthen our marriage—which I'm quickly coming to the conclusion is more fragile than I thought." His mouth was a slash of anger, rage turning his eyes a midnight black. His voice had not risen the whole time he had spoken, but the menacing calm in his words struck her with its violent force.

But the anger and pride in Kendall's expression equaled Drake's and she turned swiftly from him, walking toward the bathroom. "I need to go to the studio. I will be starting class tomorrow morning. Spring season opens in three weeks. As it is I have my work cut out for me." At the door to the bathroom, though, Kendall's anger melted some and she twisted around to face Drake.

He had retreated behind the stony shield that he so often wore, masking from her his inner thoughts. His face was carved with an iron hand, his body cast in a steel mold.

"Please understand, Drake, that I want to go on a honeymoon in June. I have my obligations to the company and Daniel."

"And what about your obligations to your husband?"

"Your demands are unreasonable," she fired back at him, her rage descending in full force again.

"Are they?" With that he swung around on his heel and strode from the room, the door closing so quietly behind him.

But the whispering sound echoed through Kendall's mind, and she couldn't help wondering if more than the bedroom door had been closed on her.

## *CHAPTER NINE*

The morning newspaper blocked Kendall's view of Drake as she tried to eat her breakfast. Sips of coffee scalded a path down her throat, her hand gripping the cup in a tight clasp that spoke of her inner tension.

She had been married for ten days and except for the nighttime, when Drake made love to her fiercely and demandingly, she had to remind herself that they were husband and wife. She had started class the previous week and rehearsals two days before and was very busy preparing for the opening of the spring season. But it was Drake who was gone most of the time on business, not she.

Exasperated by the silence between them, Kendall finally asked, "Will you be able to get away to go to the airport with me this afternoon to see Cara and Michael off?"

Slowly Drake lowered the paper barrier and measured her with an unsettling level look. "I should be the one to ask that question of you, shouldn't I?" came the dry reply after another of those lengthy pauses that were quickly eating away at Kendall's fragile nerves.

"I don't have a rehearsal this afternoon after three."

"How nice for Cara," Drake said sarcastically.

Kendall balled her hands into tight fists, her fingernails embedded in the palms. "Even if I had, she's my only sister and I would have missed the rehearsal to see her off. Remember, she'll be gone for two years." Her voice had hardened into an irate tone, fire snapping to life in her blue eyes. "Please, would you reconsider sending Michael to Alaska?" She hated the pleading tone of her voice, but she had to ask one last time.

Drake neatly folded the newspaper and laid it on the dining room table, as though he were extremely tired and only wanted to escape her. Standing, he completely ignored her question as he immobilized her with his unwavering gaze and said, "Yes, I'll be able to go to the airport with you. I'll pick you up at the studio at three thirty." Then he strode from the dining room, leaving an uneasy quiet in his wake.

Kendall started to rise from her chair to run after him, but her pride halted her in frozen silence. That morning nine days before when he had shut the door to their bedroom, he had indeed shut the door to himself as well. She had tried to reach beyond the barricade he had erected around himself and explain her actions and feelings, but it was always there between them, firmly entrenched, one he continually reinforced each day they were married.

Again anger rose within her. If he had taken the time to get to know her, he would have realized his request for a honeymoon was impossible for her. She wasn't the type of person who could turn her back on her responsibilities or her obligations. Daniel and the Manhattan Ballet Company had given her the opportunity to fulfill her lifelong dream. Yes, she had made a commitment to Drake, too, but she still felt he was being unreasonable about the honeymoon. Was it that important *when* they took the honeymoon? She had every intention of going in June. Why couldn't he wait a couple of months?

With a heavy sigh Kendall pushed her plate away and stood, without having eaten a thing. Glancing at her watch, she realized she only had thirty minutes to get to the dance studio before the company class began.

Hurriedly she gathered up her dance bag and made her way to the elevator. Outside she hailed a taxi, then leaned back and tried to relax without much success.

At the dance studio Kendall quickly readied herself for class and the rehearsal to follow. She determinedly blocked everything from her mind except the dance steps she had been asked to perform. Once she had made the mistake of allowing Drake to interfere in her concentration and she had ended up injuring her ankle. That, she vowed to herself, couldn't happen again.

But throughout the day, first in class and then in rehearsal with Greg, she had trouble keeping that vow. Drake kept flitting across her mind at the oddest times, but luckily she didn't hurt herself.

After rehearsal Kendall was dressed and ready to leave to meet Drake when Greg stopped her in the hallway. "Tell Cara I'll miss her. I wish I could go with you to the airport, but I still have to rehearse for *La Valse.*"

Her heartbeat slowed at the mention of the ballet she had badly wanted to dance. "How's it going?"

"Melinda is good. We partner well together, but I've stopped pursuing her on a more personal level. When Andre returns, alas, I will be forced to give you up, so it is nice to have someone else who I'm comfortable dancing with."

Kendall rested a hand on his arm. "I'm glad. Really I am," she added at his surprised look.

"I think you mean it." Greg paused for a moment, then asked, "By the way, have you heard from Andre?"

"He'll be back in five weeks and will be able to dance the last half of the season with the company. I don't know how he manages it. I don't think I would like living out of a suitcase as much as he does."

"That's the price of fame, my dear. The more famous you become, the more in demand you are. How will Drake feel about that, Kendall? You know it will be only a matter of time before you're touring as much as Andre. Take for instance the tour this summer to Europe. . . ."

"I wish I could, Greg, but right now I'm five minutes late to meet Drake." Kendall managed the semblance of a smile as she spun around and headed for the elevator.

She didn't want to think about the tour to Europe. She hadn't told Drake about it and she wasn't sure if he knew. He hadn't mentioned it to her, so she suspected he didn't. The tour didn't involve the company, only Andre and herself. The plans for it had been settled six months before. How would Drake feel about it? Dread encased her, for she knew she would have to tell him soon. But she would pick the right time, when he wasn't so angry with her.

Drake was standing by TI's chauffeured limousine, waiting for her with the door open. She slid into the intimate confines, mustering a smile of greeting for a granite-faced Drake.

Something was wrong. Kendall could feel it in the tense lines of his body as his arm and leg pressed into hers. She ventured a glance at him and met the forbidding look on his face.

"Drake, what's wrong?" Kendall laid her hand on his arm, silently beseeching him to answer her. The corded muscles beneath her fingertips flexed in tight readiness, as though he were a hunter instantly becoming alert at the first sign of danger.

"Nothing," he hissed through clenched teeth.

Somehow she knew this had nothing to do with her. He had been displeased with her this past week, but this was different. Rage burned in the depths of his eyes, a fury even he couldn't mask.

"Please, Drake, I want to share what's bothering you. I am your wife."

He looked at her with sardonic regard, one eyebrow lifting as though he challenged that assertion. "If you must know, Kendall, I will be leaving this evening for two weeks."

"Why?" The simple question came out on a rush of air. His look had raked her, strangling every breath she took.

"It seems my competitors are playing dirty and I have to fly to Tulsa, Dallas, and Houston to repair the damage." His words were clipped out in a savage voice, effectively dismissing any further discussion of the subject.

As Drake stared straight ahead, lost in his own thoughts, Kendall fought the strong impulse to reach out and smooth the deep lines from his brow. She felt his anger and concern deep within her and wished there was a way she could help ease his worry. But he didn't want it, having again cut her off.

Battling her own jumbled thoughts, Kendall stared out the window at the quickly passing scenery as they left Manhattan behind them on the long ride to Kennedy Airport. Drake's deep sigh pulled her attention to him, and before a cool mask of indifference had fallen into place, she saw a puzzling look in his eyes, as if the weight of running Taylor Industries was taking its toll.

Without thinking, Kendall touched his clean-shaven jaw, recalling a time he had made love to her recently with the scratchy feel of a day's growth of beard scraping her skin. His sandpaper cheek had been in direct contrast to the gentle ministration of his hands, which had left nothing on her body untouched, unloved.

Drake seized her stroking hand in a viselike grip, stilling its movements. For a charged moment he held her hand only a breath away from his mouth, then with light whispering kisses he touched each finger, her palm, the back of her hand, with his lips.

Kendall dissolved against his sinewy hardness, her body weak. His arms went about her and dragged her across his lap, his lips clinging to hers in a sweet desperation. While his mouth tasted hers, his hand cupped her breast.

She arched beneath the roving hand as it sampled the delights first of one breast, then the other; her nipples tautened under the singeing touch. Her body burned with her need for him. Gone from them was the anger of the past week and now all that stood between them were wounded pride and desperate emotion.

"Oh, Drake, love me," Kendall moaned against his mouth before seeking the feel of his lips on hers again in an urgent longing.

"Babe, I wish I could." Drake lifted his head, reluctantly loosening his firm embrace. "But this isn't the place to love you the way I want to."

His low chuckle propelled her upward to scan their surroundings. The limousine was pulling into the airport, and all of a sudden a lonely emptiness engulfed Kendall.

"You won't be back for opening night?"

"No," he answered as the limousine pulled to a stop in front of the terminal that Cara and Michael would be leaving from. "In fact, after seeing your sister and Michael off, I'll be leaving for Tulsa."

Her heart plummeted. Not only would she be watching

her sister leave this evening, but also her husband. The feeling of loneliness sharpened into a dull pain.

"Can't you wait until tomorrow morning?" She knew before she asked the question what the answer would be. And strangely, the feeling flirted through her that she had no right to ask him to stay one more night just because she couldn't bear to spend it alone.

For the next hour Kendall sank deeper into depression as she saw first Michael and Cara off for Alaska, then Drake for Tulsa. Tears welled in her eyes and spilled down her cheeks as his Learjet disappeared down the runway. Suddenly the next two weeks stretched before her in a prospect of dismal despair. Even thinking about opening night couldn't bring a smile to Kendall's face. Drake wouldn't be there to share it with her.

Kendall stood next to Andre on the stage and curtsied to the tremendous applause of the audience. With a strange sense of relief she moved off the stage toward the elevator that would take her to her dressing room. This was the last performance for the spring season and tomorrow morning she and Drake would finally be going on their belated honeymoon to Kauai.

Andre laid a hand on her arm to stop her from entering her dressing room. Kendall's hand dropped away from the doorknob. Ever since Andre had returned to the company five weeks before, there had been an added passion to her dancing. He had taught her much about ballet and most of all the importance of being in tune with her partner.

Even as Kendall turned to face Andre, though, she couldn't help thinking that maybe his presence wasn't the reason her dancing had become more emotional, more fiery. Drake had also returned a little over five weeks ago, his business trip evolving into a five-week odyssey that had taken him all over the world. Drake hadn't discussed his business problems much with her on his daily calls from the various cities he had visited, nor when he had returned to New York. He had declared they were behind him and he didn't want to dwell on them.

Kendall had missed Drake terribly, her ache of loneliness growing into a raging need for him, and when he had excluded her from part of his life, it had hurt a great deal. She had said nothing, though, praying instead that there would come a time when they would share everything, the disappointment as well as the joy. That was what marriage was all about. Thankfully, though, he exhibited none of the strained feelings toward her that he had displayed before his business trip.

"I have to tell you, Kendall, you were great tonight. The ballet fans will well remember this evening's performance of *Swan Lake.*" Andre bent and kissed her on the cheek, his voice soft and warm. "I hope I'll see you at Daniel's party to celebrate the end of another successful season. I must say I'm curious as to what your husband looks like."

Drake had been very busy at his office since his return, trying to catch up on the work that had piled up during his business trip. Having wanted nothing to interfere with their planned honeymoon, he hadn't been able to attend any performances. But he had been out in the audience tonight and that knowledge had spurred her to greater heights than she had thought possible.

"We'll be there, Andre. And I promise I will introduce you two. I do think it is about time my husband met my dancing partner."

"Is there a reason you kept him a well-guarded secret?" Amusement was heavy in Andre's voice.

"Jealous?" Kendall teased, turning and opening the door to her dressing room.

She glanced back to see the laughing warmth etched in Andre's expression as he started for his own dressing room, and she offered Andre a matching smile. The smile stayed on her lips as she twisted about to enter her dressing room.

The cold look of fury on Drake's face paralyzed her in mute fear. For endless moments she stood rooted to the floor, her legs unable to move forward into the dressing room.

His deadly quiet voice broke the spell of anger that had leaped across the room and spun about her in a tight shroud. "Please, my dear, come in and shut the door."

His face no longer registered any emotion, making him appear even more menacing. Kendall closed the door and advanced into the room, her legs trembling from exhaustion but most of all from that look she had caught on Drake's face as he had watched Andre walk away from her.

Her breath froze in her throat. Drake half sat, half leaned, on her dressing table, folding his arms casually, too casually, across his broad chest. In that moment he looked every inch the powerful, successful magnate he was, capable of destroying a person with just a few sentences. The intimidating set of his shoulders and the unbending lines of his face italicized the underlying anger he was, at least for the moment, keeping a tight rein on.

Kendall sank onto her stool, catching a glimpse of herself in the mirror before her. An ashen pallor had stolen into her cheeks, making her dark blue eyes seem larger than they really were. She quickly pulled herself together and lifted her defiant gaze to the icy barrenness of his.

They stared at each other for a long time, the very air about them vibrating with their heightened emotions. He unfolded his arms and dropped them to his sides, his hands gripping the tabletop. Kendall's gaze followed the movement and the intense thread that invisibly bound them together cracked, then broke like fragile glass.

"I'm sorry we're going to have to disappoint your Andre, but we're not going to Daniel's party."

The harsh words lashed out at Kendall, a knifelike awareness of his sudden closeness ripping through her. Her thoughts raced wildly in an attempt to understand Drake's strong reaction. Over the last few weeks she remembered the unusually remote attitude he adopted when she'd begin to talk about a rehearsal or a night's performance with Andre. Then she recalled his accusation the first night he had stood before her in this very dressing room about her having had an affair with Andre to further her dancing career in the company.

Kendall straightened on the stool and sent him her own chilling look. "If you don't want to go, fine. But I am going to the party."

Fingers like talons whipped out and gripped her by her upper arms, bringing her dangerously close to his lean strength. "I'm not leaving this theater without my wife, and if I have to kidnap her, I will."

A warning sounded in Kendall's mind at the steel control in Drake's voice, barely leashed, and suddenly the fight and the strength drained out of her. She was so tired from dancing the long ballet that evening that she almost swayed against him.

Wearily she tried to explain. "Drake, Andre is just my partner and a good friend. That's all."

"I'm not blind or deaf, Kendall. I saw the look he gave you and I heard him. He cares a great deal about you and you're mine."

Kendall twisted away from him. "Of course he cares. A good partnership is based on how much you know of the other, not only how your partner dances but his moods, his strengths and weaknesses, too."

As though he hadn't heard her, Drake commanded, "Get dressed. We're going home."

"No!" She stood her ground, her arms ramrod straight at her sides, as the hard impact of her eyes drilled relentlessly into him. "I'm going to the party and I hope you'll come with me."

Their gazes battled, then suddenly Drake shrugged, as if he no longer cared what she did. "Suit yourself. I'm going home. It's been a hectic, long month and the flight to Hawaii is many hours."

In three strides he was across the room and at the door. "Good night, Kendall," he murmured in a weary voice.

Kendall stared at the closed door until her eyes burned. In her heart it was hard to blame Drake for his reaction to Andre. It was hard for a nondancer to understand the intimate working relationship that existed between partners. And she and Andre had been partners for four years.

Exhausted, Kendall collapsed onto the stool, her eyes closing. At the moment she couldn't endure the thought of facing a roomful of happy, cheerful people at Daniel's party. Any thoughts of celebrating had fled with the scene between her and Drake. At one time not too long ago she had promised herself that if they had problems they would work them through and that she wouldn't run away again from them.

With her mind made up, she quickly undressed, showered, then dressed in her street clothes. She would go home and they would talk about Andre. Suddenly a thought struck Kendall. The tour to Europe! She hadn't told Drake about it yet and now she didn't know when she could. If he was jealous now, what would he do when he found out about the tour with Andre? While they were in Hawaii, she would show him how much she loved him and make him understand about Andre; then she would tell him. Drake had been right at the beginning of their marriage. They had needed some time completely alone to reacquaint themselves with each other in order to weather the rough times that always hit a marriage. No matter how close two people were, there had to be a firm base to build their marriage on. Theirs had been erected on quicksand.

The penthouse was dark when Kendall arrived home. She made her way up the stairs to their bedroom, and upon entering it, she was assailed by the fragrance of the bouquets of yellow roses that filled the room. Then she noted a table by the terrace doors, set intimately for two. A dim light on the bedside table was the only illumination in the room. He had done all this for her!

Kendall's gaze swung from the table, with its bucket of champagne sitting in melting ice, to Drake, who was coming into the room from the bathroom, toweling his hair dry, his naked body powerful, muscular, and magnificent.

Momentarily stunned by her appearance, he slowly lowered the towel, his hair still damp, his movements cautiously slow. Their eyes locked across the wide expanse of the room, and Kendall felt as if she would suffocate from the devastatingly compelling inspection that he boldly swept down her body. The probing flames of his eyes cindered any resistance she might have had, and with slow, deliberate strides he crossed the room toward her.

Glancing around at the roses, and then at the table that had indicated Drake's plans for their own very private celebration, Kendall couldn't find the voice to bring up Andre. Her love for Drake swelled within her and she smiled.

A devilishly wayward grin softened the chiseled lines of his face as he observed the direction of her glance, and then her smile. "I wanted to surprise you and start our honeymoon a little early."

Her heart pounded, her pulse shooting through her at a dizzying speed. For the life of her she couldn't think of a thing to say, her gaze riveted upon the burning warmth of his features as his eyes took her in with leisured thoroughness.

"I'm glad you came home, babe. And I'm sorry about earlier. All I could think of was that I didn't want to share you for one minute longer with anyone else and especially with Andre. He's seen you more than I have for the last five weeks."

Drake held his hand out in invitation and hers settled into his, the touch igniting her own flaring passion. Then, as though their unquenchable desire had exploded at the same time, he hauled her to him, his lips crushing into hers with a searing bolt that catapulted through her like a shooting star blazing across the midnight sky.

## CHAPTER TEN

Pushing away from her face hair dampened by physical exertion and the high humidity, Kendall rolled her head, massaging her neck as she positioned herself on the huge rock to catch the warm, fragrant breeze. She and Drake had been climbing along the Napali coast for several hours and had finally stopped for a well-deserved break.

"I know I'm in good physical condition, but I hope that we reach the place you want to camp at soon," Kendall said, exhaling a rush of air.

"Remember it was your idea to see the untamed wilderness of this part of the island." Deep lines of laughter sprayed outward from his dark eyes. "Your curiosity got the better of you, didn't it? When you heard there were no roads into this part of the island, you just had to see what was here."

"In that respect I'm not disappointed, Drake. Just look around you. It's so different from New York, or for that matter Tulsa or Grand Lake." Kendall gestured with a wide sweep of her right arm.

Lush greenery surrounded them with glimpses of a glittering blue ocean below, striking against the cliffs that comprised a great deal of the northwestern coastline of

Kauai. It was raw, primitive nature at its best, Kendall decided, tilting her head back to let the sun bathe her face.

She hadn't realized until they had reached Kauai seven days before that she had needed to escape everything having to do with dancing and New York, and to effect a complete change of scenery. When she had heard of this part of the island, she instantly thought of their total isolation, nothing but her and Drake and the beauty of nature as their backdrop.

For the past week they had sunbathed, swum, or explored the island during the daytime while at night they had recaptured the wildly exciting abandonment of their weekend at Grand Lake. But still Kendall hadn't found the time to tell Drake about the tour to Europe with Andre. She desperately hoped that sometime during the next three days the opportunity would arise. If she could be alone with Drake, giving him her complete, undivided attention, maybe he wouldn't mind the tour as much as she feared he would. That thought kept playing through her mind as they stood and began hiking again.

Two hours later Drake and Kendall arrived at the beach they had planned to set up camp on. It was engulfed by high cliffs on three sides and the ocean on one, pounding against the shore. And, Kendall thought with a delicious shiver moving up her spine, it was very private, with no one else around.

Standing in the middle of the beach, Kendall dropped her knapsack and breathed deeply of the tang of the ocean. "Oh, this is beautiful. I'm glad your friends told you about this place, Drake."

Drake came up behind her and encircled her in his arms, pulling her back against him. "So am I. I've enjoyed the house we had on the beach, but I think I'm going to enjoy this even more. I don't have to share you with my friends or anyone else for three whole days." His low seductive chuckle tantalized her. "I'm warming to this idea of yours more and more."

His breath tickled her neck; tingling quivers flooded her senses, causing her to sway back even more. She grew weaker every second he held her to him, his light nibbles along her neck and shoulder her complete undoing. Turning within his embrace, she ended his sensual taunts with an ardent kiss, her tongue seeking the dark recesses of his mouth while his hand trailed down her back.

They ended up on the beach, entwined in each other's naked limbs, a desperation that had been lacking in the past now entering their lovemaking. Their union was frenzied, a fierce oneness that still stunned Kendall when, afterward, she lay in his arms, her head resting on his shoulder.

"I'd been wanting to do that all morning long. It was pure torture for me to follow you along that path, watching those hips sway back and forth, and not ravish you then and there. I can't seem to get enough of you, babe." The last sentence was breathed into her ear with a sexy growl rumbling deep in his chest.

A slow, contented smile inched across Kendall's features. It felt wonderful to be loved so absolutely, to be desired so totally. She savored the blissful moments within his embrace, their gazes drinking in the peacefulness of the beach, the call of a bird in the distance, the rhythmic lapping of the ocean.

During the last week she and Drake had caught up on each other's pasts, and Kendall had felt their bond strengthen. They were still very independent, making it difficult for them to admit their needs to each other, but it was a good beginning. *Then, why don't you tell him now about the tour?* her conscience questioned.

Drake reluctantly broke the silence. "I guess we ought to get on our feet and set up camp before nightfall."

"Yes, I suppose." Kendall hated to move. Drake had been right. They should have come on a honeymoon two months ago. The feelings he was creating within her were pure ecstasy. She had never felt so close to another human being, not even Andre or Greg, as she had with Drake this past week. She pushed away the nagging question to be faced at a later date.

"You know, woman, if you hadn't tempted me so much on the path back there, I wouldn't have sand covering me from head to toe. Next time we must remember in our lustful longing to lay a blanket down first."

His laugh warmed Kendall, and she snuggled closer, teasing him with feather-light brushes over his damp and sandy chest. "Let's take a shower in the waterfall that we passed back up on the cliff."

Kendall rose and tried to wipe some of the sand from her body, but most of it clung to her damp skin. Drake fumbled in her knapsack and tossed her her cover-up.

"Wear this just in case someone happens along."

Kendall shrugged into the cover-up, then headed for the path that led up the cliff, saying over her shoulder in a flippant voice, "Let's just face it, Drake Taylor. If I didn't cover up, we'd never take that shower."

Drake sat up lazily, an impish grin on his dark features. "So you don't think I can keep my hands off you."

At the beginning of the path Kendall turned, planting her hands on her hips, and nodded.

He tipped back his head and laughter filled the quiet of the beach. "You're right, my love. I can't." In one quick effortless movement he was on his feet and closing the distance between them in a burst of energy.

Kendall threw her arms up as if to ward off Drake, her own laughter mingling with his. She saw the devilish intent deep within his eyes and said breathlessly, "Don't you dare, Drake Taylor."

"Woman, you know I can never pass up a dare." And he plunged into her, tackling her and sending them both down on the sand.

Her short cover-up exposed the slenderness of her legs and the satiny smoothness of her thighs. Drake's gaze fastened upon her flushed face, then roamed lower until it rested upon her thighs. The banked flames in his eyes flared into a burning need again, his penetrating regard electrifying her senses, and they came together wildly, passionately.

Later, as they were showering finally under the small waterfall, they ended up in a water fight and a wrestling match on the lush green natural carpet, with Drake easily winning, and their laughter echoing off the cliffs.

That first day set the tone for the next two days. Sitting on the beach on a large blanket, with her legs drawn up, Kendall watched the sky become tinted with the colors of a dying day. Drake was at their waterfall shaving away a three days' growth of beard while she had stayed behind to clean up their dinner dishes. With sadness Kendall thought about having to return to "civilization" the following afternoon.

She still had avoided telling him about the tour, shoving it to the back of her mind each time she thought about it. She hadn't wanted to spoil this adventure, she had kept telling herself, but the time had now come when she had to face the problem. When they returned to New York in a few days, she would have to start rehearsing with Andre after her usual daily class. She couldn't put it off any longer, she realized with a heavy sigh, a fine-tuned tension flowing over her to make her stiff with apprehension.

Kendall closed her eyes and rested her head on her knees, allowing the peace of her surroundings to seep into her soul and relax her tense body. A whispering touch grazed her cheek and her eyes snapped open to gaze into the sensual depths of Drake's.

"I hated to disturb you, babe, but that position would be most uncomfortable to fall asleep in." A roguish gleam had made his eyes bright like newly polished gems. He caressed her cheek with the back of his hand, stroking gently as his gaze devoured her. "I can think of several better ways to fall asleep."

"Would one of those ways be in your arms?" Laughter showered her question, and again she found herself lost in the bottomless abyss of his eyes, all rational thoughts fleeing her mind except Drake and what his lovemaking did to her.

Mock surprise flickered over his features. "Am I that transparent?"

"I'm afraid so."

"Oh, well, then, enough of this game-playing. Let's get down to serious business."

Drake gently shoved her back onto the blanket and covered her partially with his body, one leg thrown over hers to trap her in a snare of pure sensuality. His hands reverently brushed her hair from her face before his mouth came down upon hers in a kiss of fire and hunger.

"Oh, babe, I'm so glad we're going to have most of the summer to explore each other in depth. I want to know every minute thing about you. Your likes, dislikes, your innermost thoughts. Thank God the company doesn't have much planned this summer for you."

His soft breath touched her brow as he murmured what he would do with their spare time, shockingly wonderful things that caused Kendall to blush. Through the haze of delight he was wrapping her in, her rational side surfaced for a few brief seconds to warn her to speak now of the tour. But words of explanation lodged in her throat and again she dismissed what she knew she must do at a later time when he wasn't taking her clothes off and searching every inch of her body with tantalizing strokes.

Warm, tender, persuasive lips wandered where his hands had been only seconds ago, then returned to her own lips to command her sweet surrender. Kendall probed the thickness of his hair, pressing him closer and closer until nothing separated them except his clothes.

A coldness spread through her when he stood to shed his cutoff jeans, the sheer beauty of him evident in the moonlight that highlighted his leanness. But as quickly as the coldness had bored into her, it vanished when he again joined her on the blanket, cradling her in the shelter of his arms.

His burning urgency struck a chord in her own body, his tongue sliding into her mouth, circling it, and sensually exploring the soft inside. The fiery awareness of his hands on her breasts, teasing them into tautness, sent a rampaging blaze through her veins.

Kendall relished the weight of him on her, the husky whispers of his needs, his love, his scent, all of which she had come to know so well. A fervent wave of unbelievable pleasure roared through her, equaling the sound of the surf as it hammered against the beach. It transported her to a high plateau where Drake and she blended into one identity and her senses clamored for more and more, and she took and gave of herself as never before.

Lying exhausted within the circle of his arms, the rays of the moon covering them in a silvery light, Kendall brushed her fingers across his mouth, outlining it before tracing his firm jawline.

After what they had just shared, she would tell him about the tour, but for a few more minutes she wanted to savor the heated rapture they had given each other.

"I wouldn't mind building a hut here on the beach and dropping out of civilization for a few years with you," he said.

His husky growl in her ear was like a caress, arousing her even after she had been so thoroughly sated. "What would we do in the winter months when the ocean reclaims this beach until the late spring?"

He waved his hand in the air. "That's just a minor detail we can work out later."

His voice was pitched to a low, sexy level that produced images of them running in the surf or showering under the waterfall naked as though they were Adam and Eve in the Garden of Eden. If there was a place on Earth that was like the Garden, then surely this was it, Kendall decided, propping herself up on an elbow, her fingers tangling in the hair on his chest. And she also realized there would be no better time to tell Drake about the tour than at that moment.

"Drake, as much as I wish I could build that hut with you, I can't."

Before she could say another word, Drake imprisoned her wandering hand and flipped her over on her back, pinning her arms above her head. "Darling, as much as I wish I could build that hut with you, I can't, either. The next couple of months Taylor Industries is going to keep me hopping."

The only subject they hadn't discussed much was their future plans, especially regarding their demanding careers. Now the subject had to be broached.

The shadows of night hid from Drake the troubled darkness in Kendall's eyes, but her body tensed beneath him. The tender grip on her wrists loosened and he pushed himself up and away from her.

"There's something you're not telling me, isn't there?" Suspicion hardened his voice slightly.

Drake sat up on the blanket, his back to her, his arms dangling over his raised knees. He stared out at the ocean, a dark void that stretched for endless miles.

"Out with it, Kendall. Something's bothering you."

"When we return to New York, I must start preparing for a tour to Europe that begins in a month's time."

"The company isn't going to Europe." His voice was iced with a chilling cold.

"They aren't, but Andre and I are. It's been planned for over eight months now." Kendall laid a hand on his shoulder, the muscles beneath her fingers stiffening with the touch.

Drake surged to his feet and quickly donned his cutoff jeans. He thrust Kendall's shorts and T-shirt at her and commanded, "Get dressed."

She recoiled from the whip of his voice, a blazing fury shattering the air about her as if it were shards of glass spiking her. Rising, she said, "Drake, please let me explain about the tour."

He faced her with all his anger apparent in the rigid lines of his body. Even in the moonlight Kendall could see the lethal force of his expression, which was echoed in his voice.

"What's there to explain, Kendall? You've known about this tour for months, since we've been married, and yet you neglected to tell me until now. Why, my dear? Is your guilty conscience beginning to bother you?" His scorn ricocheted off the high cliffs that sheltered them from the world, coming to strike again and again at Kendall.

Her fingers ached to smooth away the anger that lined his face so savagely, but she kept her distance, knowing the contempt he would show her if she moved any closer. He was hurting inside and she berated herself for having been a coward with him for the second time in her life. The anger in his voice was as impenetrable as stone and she wasn't sure how to tear the barrier down. But somehow she had to try and make him understand.

Kendall dressed while Drake walked toward their tent. He was like a time bomb, methodically ticking away, and she was subconsciously bracing herself for the explosion as she followed him into their tent, where he had already lit a lantern.

Kendall stood in the doorway, a sharp-edged tension ribboning tautly through her. Drake lay on his sleeping bag with his arms crossed behind his head, staring up at the ceiling of the tent. His face was void of emotion.

"I'm sorry, Drake. I didn't start out keeping this tour a secret from you. It's just that every time I started to tell you about it I couldn't find the words. I can't back out and I knew how much you were looking forward to our having some time alone together this summer."

Something flickered in his eyes as he propped himself up on one elbow, his rugged features twisting into a cynical smile. "You're damn right I was looking forward to my wife traveling some with me this summer. I have to be away from New York a lot in the next few months and I thought maybe I would be lucky enough to have you accompany me some of the time. I was a fool to have thought that." The last sentence was spat out in self-disgust.

"Are you jealous of Andre?" Her own anger was beginning to sizzle through her veins.

"You got it, babe. You two share something special. I can see it when you dance together. He's a part of your life in a way I will never be." Drake turned away from Kendall and added, "Good night. Turn off the lantern when you're ready to go to bed."

She had been the fool, not Drake, to think they could work out their problems when they hadn't taken the time to become good friends, only lovers. This past week they had taken the first steps in really getting to know each other, but now it was as if all their progress had been for nothing. Would Drake ever forgive her for having placed her dancing first six years before? For that was still behind all his anger now.

## *CHAPTER ELEVEN*

Kendall put the last place-card by the crystal water glass, then surveyed one last time the dining room table, set for fourteen, before walking from the room and heading for her bedroom. Drake would be home from his trip to Tulsa, the third one in two weeks, at any moment.

Her steps were leaden as she neared their bedroom. They had returned from Hawaii three weeks before and the atmosphere between them was definitely chilly. They had seen very little of each other since their belated honeymoon. She had been rehearsing for the tour, while Drake had been busy with TI, commuting back and forth between Tulsa and New York.

Kendall moved into their bedroom and across it to the bathroom, where she disrobed and stepped into the shower, letting the water rush through her fingers until it had achieved a comfortable temperature. The warmth hammered at her and she relished the water's heated fingers as they massaged some of the tension from her.

She prayed this dinner party would go well. She had to prove to Drake that she cared about his business and wanted to be a part of it. If he could see how much time, of which she had had little to spare lately, she had spent on this business dinner, then maybe he wouldn't be so angry that she hadn't told him about the tour sooner. He felt she was trying to exclude him from part of her life, to hide something from him. That simply wasn't true, but she hadn't done much to convince him when they were first married, she had to admit to herself.

Kendall was toweling herself dry when the bathroom door opened and Drake entered the steamy room, his face lined with exhaustion. Kendall wanted to go to him and ease the tired look from his features with her fingers, but his hard gaze flicked over her once before he turned to shave, effectively dismissing any need for her concern.

But still Kendall couldn't help asking as she shrugged into her robe, "Was the trip successful?"

"Possibly," was his clipped reply.

He smoothed shaving cream over the lower part of his face and, without another word to her, began to shave. But in the mirror he watched Kendall leave the bathroom, pride stamped into her features, her slim body graceful as she moved.

Why couldn't he tell her what he was thinking, feeling? During the past three weeks he had wanted to many times, but he hadn't. He had never been a person who could easily talk about his inner feelings and Kendall had hurt him deeply by excluding him again from an important part of her life, just as she had six years before.

Each time he returned from a business trip he kept thinking about how he had wanted her to go with him. Dammit! He knew he was being unrealistic about wanting her by his side, but she was so damned independent. He didn't feel she really needed him, and that thought lanced deeply and painfully into him.

"Which dress do you think I should wear, Drake?"

Kendall appeared in the doorway, holding up two evening gowns.

Drake's gaze met Kendall's through the reflection in the mirror. Slowly he twisted about and said with a shrug, "Either one will be fine, I'm sure." Then he turned back to finish shaving.

*Stay calm,* Kendall told herself over and over as she dressed in a black silk gown with a slit up one side. It accentuated her slender legs and small waist and was a perfect foil for her ivory complexion, tanned slightly from the days in Hawaii.

But when Drake reentered the bedroom to put on his three-piece gray suit, the atmosphere crackled between them as if there were an electric storm in the room. She hurriedly finished applying her makeup, wanting to escape Drake's presence. Somehow she had to assemble her cool poise tonight if this dinner party was to be a success. Her nerves were frayed from long hours of exhausting rehearsals and classes and most of all from wondering where their relationship was heading.

"I'm going on downstairs to check with Marianne about dinner." Kendall stood on shaky legs, gripping the dressing table for a few seconds to steady herself, her emotions churning within her.

"I'm sure Marianne has everything under control. She's been doing this kind of thing for years." Drake knotted his tie, his jerky movements betraying his anger, his tone clearly implying that he had more confidence in Marianne than in her.

From years of striving to be the best in her profession, Kendall's fighting spirit surfaced and suddenly she had had enough of Drake's giving her the cold shoulder. "Damn you, Drake Taylor! I've had it! How will we ever be able to work out our problems if you continue to shut me out of your life?"

Drake put his vest on, slowly buttoning it up as though stalling for time. "Shut you out of my life? Shouldn't I be asking you that question?" After jamming his arms into his suit jacket, he strode toward the door. Once there, he turned back to say, "Six years ago I wanted to include you in my life, but you had to come to New York and dance with the Manhattan Ballet Company. A few months ago I made you my wife and yet you couldn't take the time to go on a honeymoon. I didn't want you to give up your dancing, just find some time for me in your life. I'd realized we'd both changed in six years and I wanted us to become friends, to really get to know each other. I suppose I was in the wrong in insisting we marry, then get acquainted, but I was afraid you would run away again from your feelings and from me." He laughed, a sound void of any humor. "In my business I can be cold and ruthless, calculating every move I must make with extreme care, but with you I am continually making mistakes until I'm weary of even trying. For the last few months I've been fighting a very hard battle not only with my competitors, who would like to put me out of business, but on the home front as well. And suddenly I'm very tired of it all." Drake spun around on his heel and thrust the bedroom door open.

Kendall felt as if a cold bucket of water had been thrown in her face. Marriage was a two-way street and neither of them was willing to give up an inch nor any part of their independence.

Didn't he see that she needed his support for this upcoming tour? This would be the first time she would be a guest star with the best ballet companies in Europe. She needed all the emotional and physical strength she could muster. If the tour was a success, there would be more tours in the future to different parts of the world, and she would dance with the world's best, a nineteen-year-old dream come true.

She loved Drake and was determined to have both him and a career. Until a few minutes ago she hadn't realized the extreme pressure he was under with his business. He needed her support as she needed his. He didn't think she cared, so he was pulling away from her. She would start with this dinner party, and instead of rehearsing all of next week before leaving on the tour, she would go with him to Tulsa and perhaps they would be able to spend a weekend at Grand Lake.

But throughout the party they were polite strangers, Drake's dark, brooding gaze always gauging her as if she were on trial. When the last guest had left, Kendall sank down onto the couch, slipping her high heels off. All in all she had felt the evening was a success and as Drake entered the living room, she expected him to make a comment on the smoothness of the dinner party. She had spent many hours planning it, hours when she should have been working at the studio.

When Drake didn't say anything, but instead walked to the bar and fixed himself a whiskey, Kendall said, "I'll have a glass of white wine, please."

He poured her a glass of wine and handed it to her, grazing her fingers. Their gazes collided and Kendall winced at his icy regard. Quickly she took the glass and sipped the wine until nearly all of it was gone.

"I thought the party went well," Kendall said in a casual voice.

Silence.

Kendall chanced a look at Drake who was standing in front of the fireplace and staring down into the empty grate. "Didn't you?"

Drake jerked his head up and around to stare at her. "If you call putting Mr. Collins near Mr. Davidson a success, then, yes, it was."

"What do you mean, Drake?" Puzzlement furrowed Kendall's brow.

"They aren't what I would call friends and the farther they are away from each other the better for everyone. Didn't you see how forced the conversation was at my end of the table?"

"Then, why did you invite both men to the same party?"

He measured her with his cold eyes. "My dear, if I could have gotten out of it, I would have. But if you knew anything about the people I do a lot of business with, you would realize that Collins is Brad Morris's brother-in-law and junior partner. And since Brad is an important customer, I couldn't offend him and say no when he asked to bring Collins. By that time Davidson was already coming."

He had been towering over her, lecturing her as if she were a child, and Kendall's anger leaped into her eyes. She rose, so he wouldn't seem so much like a king ruling over a meek subject.

In a voice so quiet that Drake had to strain to hear, Kendall asked, "And just how was I suppose to know about this feud? I assumed since they both were coming that they were friends, not enemies."

"That's your problem, Kendall. You assume a lot."

"You're right there. I assumed you would be pleased with my efforts." Kendall whirled around and fled the living room, tears of fury and frustration tightening in her throat. She'd be damned if she would cry in front of him!

Inside their bedroom she collapsed onto the brass bed and fought back the tears. He wasn't worth it, she thought rebelliously. But she couldn't muster the conviction needed. Her eyes shimmered with her hurt emotions. Even now, as angry and frustrated as she was, he aroused her desire, her womanly need to feel totally a part of him. They hadn't made love since that night she had told him about the tour, and her body screamed its need for his touch, his possession.

The door slammed open, Drake standing in the doorway as if he were a conquering warrior returning home. He stepped into the bedroom and kicked the door closed. With slow, stalking strides he advanced on her.

"I haven't properly thanked my wife for her services."

The hard glint in his midnight-dark eyes trapped her, paralyzing her as if she were a snared rabbit. The strong lines of his features were so aggressive, definitely cynical and definitely ruthless.

But try as she might, her body wouldn't obey the command from her brain to move, until it was too late and he was kneeling on the bed, dangerously close. His arm shot out and seized her wrist, hauling her next to him.

"Since you've felt neglected, Kendall, these last few weeks, I've decided to do something about it."

His mouth closed over hers swiftly in a hard, punishing kiss. She tried to twist her head away, but he just held it still with his powerful hands. Slowly the savage onslaught of his mouth gentled, his hands no longer imprisoning but caressing the long line of her neck, the pulsating hollow of her throat.

When he pulled back slightly, the fury that had raged

earlier in his eyes was gone. More softly now his mouth settled over hers, teasing her lips apart to taste of her. Their tongues dueled, striking, then retreating, only to meet again.

His manipulating hands slid the thin straps of her gown from her shoulders and sought her firm, small breasts to taunt them with light, flicking touches. Her passion flamed into life in complete harmony with his.

"Oh, Kendall, what has happened to us? I love you, babe."

"Neither one of us has had to depend on anyone else. It isn't easy for us to admit our needs to each other." She tunneled her fingers through his thick brown hair. "I love you, Drake. Please believe that."

"Surprisingly I never doubted that, Kendall. I want us to be a family, to have children."

"Please don't rush me—us—Drake."

He answered her plea with his lips, his hands, his body speaking the love he felt for her.

Kendall disembarked from Drake's Learjet at Tulsa International and made her way to the car that Drake had left for her use. She was to meet him at the cabin on Grand Lake. He was out at an oil field that the company owned and she hoped he would be able to join her by the late afternoon. They had three days to spend together before she had to return to New York and from there depart for her five-week tour of Europe.

Kendall headed the car toward the lake, excitement building within her as she thought of their last time at the cabin. Andre hadn't been pleased that she had wanted this long weekend right before the tour, but she had insisted. It was important to her marriage. Since the dinner party the strain that had been between them had lessened some and she intended to use this weekend to obliterate it completely.

After parking the car in front of the house, Kendall put her suitcase inside the front door, then made her way toward the bluff that overlooked the lake. She spent a lazy few hours enjoying the quiet, knowing that the ensuing weeks would be hectic, with her traveling all over Europe. The strain of being a guest star was tremendous, having to fit in with a company of dancers with whom she would be unfamiliar.

Kendall took a nap when she went up to the cabin, fully expecting Drake to arrive after she had slept for an hour. But the sun set, her feeble attempt at dinner grew cold, and still there was no Drake. Worry mushroomed as images of him lying injured somewhere flashed through her mind.

At eleven the phone finally rang and Kendall jumped at the jarring sound that sliced through the silence of the house. Breathlessly she answered it, her hands trembling so badly that she had to hold it in both fists.

"Kendall, I'm sorry I couldn't get to a phone earlier, but there has been a problem that came up at the Tulsa office that I had to drive in to see about. If everything goes well, I should be at the cabin sometime tomorrow afternoon."

Relief, then anger, bolted through Kendall. But in a very calm voice she asked, "Do you realize how worried I've been these last few hours?"

"I'm sorry, but this couldn't be helped." His curt tone nullified his apology. "I'll see you when I can get there."

Kendall sat holding the phone for long minutes after he had hung up. She was trying to get a grip on her anger and to remain calm. But her valiant efforts were failing. It was all right if his business called him away but not if hers did.

Sleep evaded her until three in the morning; afterward she slept restlessly for a few hours. The sunrise was as lovely as the others she had seen at the cabin, but she found herself turning away from its beauty. Without Drake she was immune to its serenity.

At one point in the middle of the night she had seriously thought of going back to New York and her own work to prepare for the tour. But finally her heart had won that argument. He wouldn't be able to accuse her of not trying where their marriage was concerned.

Most of the following day passed without Drake appearing, and with each hour that ticked away Kendall's anger grew. She heard his car pull up out front while she was sitting on the bluff, the dusk a mantle of shadows about her. She didn't move to get up.

When she heard her name being called, she remained quiet, slowly counting to twenty, then thirty. Nothing erased the rage, though, as the sounds of his approaching footsteps produced a tightening in every muscle.

He sat down next to her on the grass, but he didn't attempt to say anything. After a few minutes of brooding silence, Kendall slanted a glance at Drake. She swerved her attention back to the dark lake below, determined not to be the first one to break the silence. If this was a contest of wills, then Drake Taylor had a surprise in store for himself, she vowed silently.

Finally Drake spoke. "I have to leave tomorrow morning, Kendall. I couldn't clear up the mess, so I have to go back to Tulsa. It will take days to straighten out this latest disaster at the Tulsa office." He started to add that he would have to fire his Tulsa manager because of his mismanagement these past six months and then take the time to search and train another manager. This branch of his business was the most important to the company overall and the dearest to his heart. But after one look at Kendall's face, set in a frown, he knew she didn't care one way or another. So he let his voice trail off into the silence of the night and waited tensely for her to comment.

"I see," was all she said after a lengthy pause. "Well, Andre will be pleased that we will be able to get another day of rehearsal in before leaving."

"I was worried you would be disappointed, but then I should have known better." Drake stood and dusted off his black pants. "I'm hungry. Do you want me to fix you anything to eat?"

She felt his presence behind her, his eyes boring into her rigid back, and she shuddered. "No, go ahead and eat without me. I'll be up later."

Throughout the rest of the evening they spoke little, and only when they retired for the night did they convey their bottled-up emotions, letting down their guard and becoming completely honest with each other through their lovemaking. Their actions spoke of their needs, their dependence on each other, but later, as they lay exhausted with spent passions, a silence hovered between them.

Drake awoke before Kendall early the next morning. He stared down at her beautiful face, his heartbeat slowing at the thought that this would be their last time together for five weeks. After dressing in jeans and a knit shirt, he strolled along the bluff, weariness in every fiber of his being. Taking a cigarette from a pack, he lit it and inhaled deeply.

He was unsure of where he stood in Kendall's life. He didn't know how he would make it through the next five weeks. Their separation over the past month had frustrated him so much that he was constantly snapping at his staff for little mistakes. His business demanded that he stay in the United States while Kendall was in Europe. If he were lucky, he might be able to clear up everything and grab a few days off to see her at the end of the tour. She especially wanted him to see her perform with the ballet company in London, but he didn't know if he would be able to get away. This was a crucial time for Taylor Industries. If everything worked as he had planned it, he wouldn't have to slave for fifteen hours a day in the near future. Then he could take more time from his business to be with Kendall. Drake paused, crushing his cigarette out with the heel of his shoe.

He had thought he could accept her dancing career, but he was finding that more difficult than he had anticipated. Ever since this tour had come up with Andre, feelings of jealousy had surfaced and were very strong now. It wasn't the relationship between Kendall and Andre as a man and woman that bothered him. It was their closeness as dancers, a friendship he envied. Andre had a kinship with Kendall that he wanted desperately. He wanted to feel that he was a necessary, important part of her life, and he didn't. Her having walked out on him six years ago still clouded his judgment where she was concerned.

When Drake returned to the cabin, Kendall was up and in the kitchen attempting to fix their breakfast. Watching her from the doorway looking so enticingly beautiful, Drake felt his resentment rise at his business and her career that were constantly driving them apart.

"Let's eat. Then I'll drive you to the airport. Robert will see that the other car is returned to the office," Drake said, sitting down at the table. His voice had been stiff, as though he didn't know quite what to say to her.

As they ate their breakfast, they talked about everything but what was really on their minds: their impending separation. Kendall played with her breakfast, her appetite dying as the fact that they would be apart for five long, miserable weeks hit her full force. Living out of a suitcase had never held a great appeal for her. This was important to her dancing career, and yet some of the excitement of the tour was dying at the thought of all those strange hotel rooms and all the unfamiliar stages she would have to dance on.

"Have you heard from Cara lately? The last I heard from Michael they were settling down nicely in Alaska," Drake said, finishing his last sip of coffee (which thankfully wasn't as bitter as the first cup Kendall had made for him).

"She thinks she's pregnant, but hasn't gone to the doctor yet."

"Is she happy about that?"

"Yes, I think she is."

"And how do you feel about it?"

"What I feel doesn't really matter. But I am happy for both of them if that's what they want. I've reconciled myself to the fact that Cara never wanted to be a dancer as much as I do and it's not a life I would wish on anyone unless she really wanted it."

In the air between them hung a silent question. How did she feel about having children? She realized Drake was almost thirty-seven years old and ready to start a family. Suddenly she had to stop and think. How did she really feel about having a baby right now? She didn't know.

## *CHAPTER TWELVE*

Drake's gaze was riveted to the stage, following his wife's every move, each dance step fusing into the next one. She was exquisite, he thought, his pulse quickening at the prospect that they would finally be together after a five-week separation. A long-distance relationship was definitely not for him. The past five weeks had been pure hell from a personal and business standpoint, but after a lot of hard work Taylor Industries was doing great. Now he wanted to devote his energies to his marriage. Kendall would be back in New York for the next six months and he wouldn't have to travel very much, if at all, for a while.

Before him Kendall was dancing with a fiery passion as Aurora in *The Sleeping Beauty.* All over Europe the critics had loved her. She had become an instant success. Instant! That would be hardly the word for all the years of work that had gone into making Kendall the ballet dancer she was today. He was so proud of her. The world could look and enjoy her dancing while she was onstage, but offstage she was his. It had taken this separation to make him see he would take her on any terms. She was the other half of him.

Silence fell as the music ended. Kendall's smile grew as she awaited her turn to curtsy. This was the last performance of the tour and Drake was in the audience, having arrived from New York late this afternoon. The past five weeks had been long and hard on her. Recently she hadn't even felt like eating, and living in strange hotels was definitely not for her. Soon she would be going home!

As the soloists were taking their bows, Kendall's smile wavered, a wave of nausea flooding her. She reached out and gripped Andre's hand for support. It was finally Andre's and her turn to take their bows, but the dimly lit theater was spinning before her. Her grip on Andre's hand tightened as a dizzy sensation assailed her.

A hush descended over the audience, the thunderous applause dying as Andre's arm went about Kendall and he led her off the stage. When they were backstage, Andre bent and picked Kendall up in his arms to carry her the rest of the way to her dressing room.

She smiled weakly up at him, but still she felt lightheaded. "Thanks. I don't know what's wrong, but suddenly I feel dizzy."

"Do you want me to call a doctor?"

"No, I'll be fine. I just need to lie down and probably eat a decent meal for a change."

Andre placed her on a lounge in her dressing room and was straightening his back when the door was thrust open. Drake quickly moved into the dressing room, concern engraved in his features, his mouth compressed into a thin line.

"What happened, babe?"

"Nothing. I'll be okay in a minute." Kendall closed her eyes to the spinning room, inhaling deep breaths, then exhaling slowly.

"I'm calling a friend of mine who's a doctor. I want him to check you out tonight." Drake's concern deepened as he stared down at Kendall's ashen features. Turning to Andre, he asked, "Will you stay with her until I get back?"

Kendall opened her eyes, saying in exasperation, "Really, you two, I will be fine in a few minutes."

"Then, humor me, Kendall. I'll be back in a minute."

When Drake returned to Kendall's dressing room, the artistic director of the English company was leaving and Kendall was now sitting up, some of her color restored.

After Andre left the dressing room, Drake said, "Anthony will meet us at the hotel. Do you feel up to changing?"

"Honestly, Drake, I'm not an invalid. Yes, I can change, and you can call your friend back and cancel that appointment. I haven't been eating much lately and a dancer's life isn't exactly a lazy one. I just overdid it. That's all." Kendall stood, her hands on her waist, her blue eyes flashing their warning.

"And as stubborn as always." Their gazes quarreled across the expanse of the dressing room. "Well, Kendall Taylor, you will see Anthony tonight whether you like it or not." His look softened and he stepped closer until there were only a few inches between them. "You are paler than you were five weeks ago."

"That might be because ballet is an indoor activity."

His fingertip brushed down her arm, sending a riot of sensations cascading through her. She hadn't been able to see Drake before the performance and suddenly she needed to be held by him, to feel the comfort of his arms about her.

Drake drew her into the circle of his arms and whispered against her hair, "Please do this for me. It would make me feel better, babe."

She nodded, relishing the subtle musky tang of him, the masculine warmth of his body next to hers. Tipping her head back, she regarded him boldly, her features shrouded with restrained passion. Slowly, ever so slowly, he bent his head toward hers, and their lips met in a glorious exhilaration.

"Do you want me to help you shower and dress?" His husky question shivered through her.

"Do you want me to see your doctor friend?"

He chuckled softly, pulling away and placing a few feet between them. "I guess you're right. If I did, we would never get to the hotel in time. And since he's coming as a favor to me, I suppose the patient ought to be there."

Kendall faced away from him, glancing back over her shoulder to say, "You can, though, unzip my gown. I won't be too long."

"Woman, you're testing my patience. I'm a starving man who sees a delicious morsel dangling in front of his eyes."

Laughter pealed from Kendall's throat. "Where's that cool, controlled façade you wear for your business associates?"

"Gone, I'm afraid."

Drake's hands settled heavily on her shoulders before drifting down to her waist, as though he were measuring her. Then reluctantly he lifted one hand to slide the zipper down, exposing her satin-smooth back to his all-consuming gaze. He eased first one strap, then the other, from her shoulders, leaning forward to kiss the tingling flesh where her straps had been, burning her with the light impression of his lips.

"You know, Anthony is a good friend and should understand a necessary delay."

Laughingly Kendall evaded Drake's touch and scurried into the bathroom. "You're impossible, Drake, but I love you anyway."

"For that delightful confession I will allow you to take a shower—alone. But beware, babe, the minute Anthony leaves you'll have your work cut out for you."

Kendall hurriedly showered and tried to dress quickly, but Drake kept getting in the way, wanting to help button this or zip up that, his hands always lingering longer than necessary.

By the time they reached their hotel, Anthony was waiting for them in the lobby. After the introductions were made, they all rode the elevator up to the suite Drake and Kendall occupied, and Anthony proceeded to examine Kendall in the bedroom.

When the doctor told Kendall she was pregnant, she sat stunned in a chair in the bedroom, the news slowly penetrating her dazed mind.

"I can't be! We took precautions. I know I couldn't take the pill, but we used other methods."

"Precautions aren't one hundred percent effective, Kendall. When you return to New York, make an appointment to see your own doctor, but from my estimations you are several months along."

Almost to herself Kendall said, "I thought it was just the excitement of this tour and the change that made me late."

"I'll send Drake in. Good night, Kendall. And congratulations to the both of you."

She hardly noticed the doctor leaving the bedroom, her shock gradually receding to be replaced by a feeling that her life was completely out of her control. She wanted a family, but she wasn't prepared for one now.

Drake was beside her immediately, a bright smile on his features that fueled her anger. "Oh, babe, that's great news! Are you feeling all right now?"

"No!" Feeling trapped, Kendall shot to her feet and quickly moved away from his heady presence. Whirling to face Drake, she said, "Well, I guess you got your way in the end after all. You'll have your family and I won't be dancing for at least a year. Why couldn't you have been satisfied with starting a family in four or five years? I've just swept triumphantly through Europe and I'm reaching the peak of my career and you want me to take off for a year to have a child. We didn't even discuss it. I had no choice in the matter!"

A vision of Melinda's triumphant smile when she should find out about Kendall's pregnancy plagued her. This was the opportunity Melinda had been waiting for. Melinda would step into her shoes without her even putting up a fight!

"I can't believe you're saying this!" Drake replied. "It takes two to tango, my dear, or haven't you heard that? Maybe my wife is having second thoughts since the tour with Andre. You've certainly seen him more than your husband lately."

Defiantly she returned his impudent look with her own unshakable one. "That was uncalled for!"

"And what you just said wasn't?" One of his eyebrows quirked upward in mockery. "Well, my dear, I'm finally admitting defeat where you're concerned. I'm returning to New York tonight and from there I'm moving my main office to Tulsa. New York isn't big enough for the both of us." Pivoting, he walked through the living room and out the door.

Wide-eyed, Kendall sank slowly into a chair, staring at

the place where Drake had been only a moment before. With a sudden dismal finality she realized he was gone for good, that their marriage was over as far as he was concerned.

In a trancelike state Kendall dressed for bed and lay in the darkened bedroom, unable to sleep. In a few blinding moments, what had she done to her life? Her career was dominating her life to the exclusion of everything else. She didn't rule her destiny, but her dancing did. She had allowed it to, making herself depend on it totally. Her dancing was important and would always be, but not all-important anymore. Being so single-minded wasn't healthy for anyone, and before long even her dancing would suffer.

She had taken advantage of Drake's love. She used to love to dance as an expression of her innermost creative self. But now she was letting her ambition color her judgment. She was dancing for other reasons that could slowly consume her and finally destroy her, leaving her a hollow shell of a woman. She was good and no Melindas would take her place within the company if she wanted otherwise.

In years to come, when she could no longer dance, what would she have left? Memories. But without some other direction in her life, it would become empty. Her world had been very limited until Drake had come along and shown her there was more to life than her dancing. She couldn't erase from her mind the ecstatic feelings he had created in her when they made love. She couldn't forget the wonderful trip to Hawaii, where she hadn't missed her dancing at all, but instead had enjoyed just being with Drake.

Cara's words on her wedding day came back to haunt

Kendall. Cara knew Michael was the man for her because she couldn't image her life without him. That was the way she felt about Drake!

But had she destroyed Drake's love completely this time? She wouldn't make the same mistake twice. This unborn child was a part of Drake and herself, a part she suddenly realized she wanted very much. Because she had never had time while she was growing up to form a close friendship in which needs and wants were exchanged, she didn't know how to communicate them very well to Drake. She had assumed because he loved her that he would know. She needed his support and her dancing, but especially his love. She wanted her life to be a blend of the two worlds. And she would tell him that.

Throwing back the sheet, she sat on the side of the bed and picked up the phone to make arrangements to fly back to New York immediately. For so many years she had been so independent that it was tough learning to depend on another person, but she was slowly coming to the conclusion that no one person could stand completely alone.

Kendall placed her suitcases on the floor inside the door to their bedroom, the room cloaked in early morning sunlight. By the sliding glass doors that led to the terrace, Drake half sat, half lay in a chair, his head leaning back on the cushion, his eyes closed. Looking at him, so vulnerable in sleep, not the ruthless businessman he could be, Kendall was swamped by all the love she felt for her husband, her eyes shining with her deep emotions.

Kendall crossed the room, pausing in front of Drake for a moment before sitting in the chair across from him and watching the even rise and fall of his chest, the hard planes of his face smoothed of worry and anger. She dreaded waking him up and seeing the anger return to his features.

Finally she rose and leaned over to brush her lips across his mouth in a gentle kiss. Instantly his eyes snapped open.

He straightened in the chair, his expression one of indifference. "What more do you want of me, Kendall?"

She sat down before her legs should refuse to support her. This was going to be one of the hardest things she had ever had to do. "You—your love," she whispered, her voice a weak thread.

"You had that and threw it back in my face. How much do you think I can take?"

All the time she was on the plane flying to New York she had thought about having Drake's child. That thought now gave her the strength to fight for his love. "Ever since I can remember, all I've ever wanted to be was a ballerina. Everything that I did was for that one goal. Then you entered my life and messed up the neat little picture I had of myself. You made me love you, commit myself to you, even though I fought it the whole way and was still fighting it until last night. When you walked out of the hotel suite, you forced me to take a good hard look at my life."

Kendall stood and restlessly prowled the bedroom, her gaze constantly straying to the brass bed. Taking in a deep calming breath, she continued. "I didn't like what I saw, Drake. I had let my career stand in the way of our marriage. I don't need to tour the world to dance. I don't even like to travel very much. Basically I'm a homebody and this tour to Europe gave me a glimpse of what Andre's life must be like. I was lonely and miserable in strange cities without you."

Kendall halted her pacing and twisted about to face

Drake, but his expression was neutral, not a flicker of emotion in his dark eyes. Her heartbeat became a slow throb, but she wouldn't stop her explanation. Too much was at stake here.

She knelt down in front of him and took his hands in hers. "I was in shock after Anthony told me I was pregnant, but since then I've had time to think and I want this baby with all my heart. I want you. I need you. I love you, Drake. I have to have your support, but most of all your love."

Tears crowded her eyes and spilled down her cheeks. "You are my passion, the soul I give to my dancing. Take you away and I will have nothing."

For an eternity Drake sat rigid in the chair, motionless, as though he hadn't heard a word she had said. Kendall couldn't stop the flow of her tears as they splashed onto their clasped hands.

"Please love me, Drake."

Drake withdrew a hand from hers and lifted it to her cheek, gently wiping away the damp trail left by her tears. "I always want to know what is in your heart, but I also want you to share what's in mine. This child means a lot to me. I've wanted a family for a long time, but, babe, I was willing to wait." A slow smile altered his features as his hands cupped her face. "But things were taken out of our hands. Can you really accept giving up a year to have our baby?"

Without any hesitation Kendall replied, "Yes. My dancing career won't end because I have a baby. Many dancers have, and have returned if they chose to. Margaret once told me it was dangerous for a dancer to allow her dancing to be everything to her. Now I can see the wisdom in that. What if my ankle injury had been worse?

Or what if in the future I injure myself and can't dance anymore? The way I was going I would have had nothing left in my life. I would have had nothing and no one to fall back on for support."

Drake drew her forward, touching his lips to hers in a tender search that flared quickly into a fiery need. "For months I've been afraid to bend for fear I would always have to bend with you. I never had to or wanted to share my life with anyone until I met you, but even then I didn't give up trying to dominate you and bend you to my will. I know that's why you ran from me six years ago and now I can't blame you for running away."

Drake pulled Kendall up onto his lap, securing her close to him. "Dancing is a very important part of you and has shaped you into the person you are today, the woman I fell in love with. How could I really expect you to give all that up and not change? I love everything about you. Last night when I saw you dance, I wanted to shout to the world you were my wife. I was so proud of you."

"That's the first time you've said that to me." Her eyes glowed with her elation.

"But it won't be the last. I may not be able to partner you on the stage like Andre or Greg, but I can in every other aspect of your life. And I can always be there as an avid fan and an emotional support for you. I don't expect you to come to work for me at TI. We can both have our separate careers, but we can both be there for each other, too."

Kendall rested her head on his shoulder, feeling content but very tired from everything that had happened in the past twenty-four hours. Then something Drake had said in the hotel suite flashed into her mind and she asked,

"What about your plan to move TI's main office to Tulsa?"

His throaty chuckle stirred the skin below her ear as he whispered, "A threat thrown out in a fit of anger."

A tremor spread over her as his hands began to roam the soft curves of her body. "Then you don't want to move the main office?"

He nipped playfully at her ear. "Not for a few years, until you're ready to retire. Then, if you want, we can make our home in Tulsa where you can work and teach with the ballet company you started out with."

Drake placed a finger under her chin and turned her head so their mouths were only a breath apart. "There is one good thing that has come out of all the problems I've had with TI lately. I've learned the art of compromise. Sometimes the benefits far outweigh what you have had to give up."

His mouth mated with hers, commanding a fevered response that she gladly gave as her slender frame melted against his solidness.

"Love me, Drake."

"That, babe, I most certainly plan on doing."

*LOOK FOR NEXT MONTH'S*
*CANDLELIGHT ECSTASY ROMANCES®*

210 LOVERS' KNOT, *Hayton Monteith*
211 TENDER JOURNEY, *Margaret Dobson*
212 ALL OUR TOMORROWS, *Lori Herter*
213 STORMY SURRENDER, *Jessica Massey*
214 TENDER DECEPTION, *Heather Graham*
215 MIDNIGHT MAGIC, *Barbara Andrews*
216 WINDS OF HEAVEN, *Karen Whittenburg*
217 ALL OR NOTHING, *Lori Copeland*